FAKECATION

ELLE RIVERS

***

Cover Art by Allie McGilberry

Edited by Kasey Kubica

Copyright © 2024 by Elle Rivers

All rights reserved.

A NOTE FROM ELLE

This novel contains topics some might find disturbing. Please note that this novel contains discussions of ADHD and medication for mental illness, cheating of spouse with a member of the family, emotional manipulation from parents, and flashbacks from an abusive partner, both physical and emotional. There is also discussion of religious manipulation. This is not intended to be indicative of *all* religion, only the hypocrisy of one particular character. The religion portrayed is not my commentary on the topic as a whole but on how it can be practiced poorly. If these topics bother you, please take care when reading this novel. If there is a warning I missed, please email me at elle@ellerivers.com and I will rectify the situation.

To anyone who feels like their mental illness makes them undeserving of love.
You deserve the world.

CHAPTER ONE

AMELIA

Summers in Atlanta were not for the faint of heart.

When Amelia's alarm went off, she groaned and lay in bed for a good ten minutes. Her AC was blowing, and yet the apartment still felt warm and muggy. It wasn't even eight yet, but she knew it was going to be a sweltering day.

She slowly got out of bed, doing her usual song and dance of finding an outfit that was both cool enough for her walk to her MARTA stop, and warm enough to keep her from freezing in the chilly office.

She wished the executives would let them work from home.

Glancing in the mirror, Amelia made sure she looked all right. Her tan skin looked decent enough that she could forgo makeup, and her dark, wavy hair fell down her shoulders in a favorable way.

She thanked her lucky stars that it wasn't frizzy today, despite the humidity.

She left her apartment on time, only to get to the downstairs door before remembering something incredibly important.

Her medication.

She cursed under her breath, swiveled on her heel, and jogged back up the stairs to her apartment. The bottle of medication lay on the counter. Amelia took one of the pills and grabbed a banana to eat on the way to work. She knew if she had forgotten it, she would be in a world of pain.

There were times when it was incredibly inconvenient to have to rely on medication to get through the day. Her last boyfriend had certainly thought it was an issue, so much so that in the years since they'd broken it off, she had never been able to forget how he'd treated her and her reliance on medication. And how the real world felt about people like her.

That was fine. Amelia liked being alone.

She left her apartment for a second time in a rush, but luckily, she didn't miss her train. She may have been sweaty and annoyed, but at least she was on time.

Amelia got to work at exactly eight. A few of her coworkers greeted her in passing. As the HR director, she was the highest-ranking employee who worked in the office building. All her actual superiors were in corporate, and communicated via video chat, unless they were in town. All the people she worked with were technically under her umbrella.

A yawn escaped her before she had even made it to her office, and she immediately changed course, heading for coffee.

The break room was up on the top floor. There were tons of refrigerators for people to store their lunches, as well as coffeepots that were usually empty. There was a sole Keurig that Amelia had brought in, so she walked over to that.

As she bent down to open a drawer to grab a K-cup, she heard chatter.

"Isn't it so sad?" a woman's voice asked. Amelia glanced over to see two women by the fridges, huddled together as they spoke.

One of them, Andrea, was an employee of hers. After starting at the same time as Amelia three years ago, Andrea remained in her original position while Amelia pursued a promotion. On the left was Dana, who worked in the customer service department.

"It really is," Dana said to Andrea. "You can just see it in his eyes. He's *so* lonely."

Amelia immediately knew who they were talking about: Daniel Anderson—the other director in the office.

"I can't believe they got a divorce," Andrea said. "They were so cute together!"

"And she is *so* pretty," Dana added. "Like, if they had babies, they would win prizes."

"Right? Such a shame, but I hope he's happier without her."

"Isn't it weird that he's single now?" Dana asked. "I mean, he's *hot*."

"Isn't he your boss?"

"Yeah, but I could make it work."

Nope.

The last thing Amelia needed to deal with was Dana causing an HR nightmare by going after her boss.

She loudly snapped the Keurig lid closed, and both women spun around with wide eyes.

"Um, hi, Amelia!" Andrea said, her face turning red.

"Good morning," Dana parroted.

"Morning, how are you two?" Amelia asked, her voice even.

"Good!" Andrea said. "Um, did you just get here?"

"Yep."

"Great!" Dana said. "Well, I need to get back to work. Mr. Anderson runs a tight ship!"

"Yep, he definitely does," Amelia muttered under her breath as Dana quickly walked out of the break room.

"Did you hear what she said?" Andrea asked.

"I did."

She laughed, nervously playing with the hem of her shirt. "I don't think Dana will actually *do* anything."

Amelia hummed. "Sure, but it's probably best not to seduce your boss, right?"

"For sure!" Andrea said. "She's just . . . being weird."

Amelia sighed. "Do me a favor and leave the poor guy alone, okay? He's going through a lot."

Andrea nodded. "I will! I mean . . . I do leave him alone. We don't really work together anyway, so why would I even be talking to him?"

Amelia didn't really know what else to say. Her coffee began to pour.

"Well, uh . . . have a good day?" Andrea called as she scurried out of the break room.

Amelia sighed again, trying to focus on her drink. But her mind wandered to Daniel and his divorce, an issue she was familiar with.

Dana was right about one thing: he was attractive. Amelia could remember her first day, when she'd seen him walking the halls. Her eyes had caught on his impressive jawline, but also his dark hair and deep brown eyes.

At the time, it didn't matter that she was still trying to get over Andrew or that Daniel was in a management position. She was looking at someone she was ridiculously attracted to.

Then she saw the ring on his finger, and that attraction had been stuffed into a box. Since then, Daniel was simply a *coworker*.

And that was how he liked to be with them all, anyway.

Daniel was quiet and reserved. He was all business, and other than his wife, no one knew a thing about him.

The only reason anyone knew what was going on was because said wife had stormed into his office to give him the divorce papers before leaving without a word. It had been so dramatic that Amelia almost confronted him about it. Employees weren't supposed to let things like this happen, and he needed to be held to the same rules as everyone else.

But Amelia took one look at his pinched eyebrows and intense frown and she knew he didn't want his wife there either. So, she quietly had the woman removed from the list of people allowed in the building.

Amelia didn't have any kind of relationship with him to be able to ask how he was doing. And she shouldn't, considering how attracted to him she'd once been.

The Keurig sputtered the last drops of brew into her mug, and Amelia forced herself back into the present moment. There needed to be no more thinking of Daniel. She had too much work to do to get lost in her own thoughts. She picked up her coffee and used a tried-and-true way to force herself to get her day started.

I am walking to my desk. I am going to sit and work. Her mantra worked until she got to the door.

"Shit!" She'd run into someone and put all of her focus on not spilling the very full cup of coffee; she hadn't even bothered to see who it was. "Sorry, I wasn't watching where I was going."

"Neither was I," a deep male voice replied.

No one else in the office had *that* voice. Her eyes slowly trailed up, and she found herself gazing at none other than Daniel himself. She could get lost in those dark eyes.

He was freshly shaven and his hair was pushed back. But this close, she could see the slight curls. She wondered what it looked like when it was free from its typical styling.

She dragged her eyes to his, only to find herself wanting to memorize their exact shade of brown. While blue eyes got all the attention, there was something about his eyes' walnut hue that kept her attention.

That was when she realized she was staring.

"Sorry," she said, putting on a smile. "I'm a bit out of it before I've had my first cup of coffee."

Amelia lifted the mug to her mouth and took a sip. She silently begged the caffeine to do its magic and make her a fully functioning person.

"Ah. I can't relate to that."

"Not a fan of coffee?" she asked.

Daniel shook his head. "More of a green tea drinker."

She felt relieved. *See?* she told herself. *We don't even have coffee in common.*

"I noticed there was someone who always got into the green tea I stock. Bigelow, right?"

"You stock it?"

"Yeah, why not? We have to have something that keeps people happy around here."

"Did you somehow convince Cheryl to pay for it?"

"It was either that or she give me a raise to pay for it myself. She chose the first option."

"I'm impressed," he said. "Then again, you've always been that way."

Amelia's heart sped up. Was he . . . *complimenting* her?

"I mean, at your job, of course," he corrected.

"Right," she muttered. She didn't know if she was relieved or disappointed at him bringing the conversation back to work. "Thank you. That's very nice of you to say."

Thankfully, another employee was speed-walking to the break room and almost ran right into them. Amelia immediately recognized her as Stacey, another of her employees.

"Whoa!" she said, blinking at them with wide eyes. "Wow, hi, Daniel, Amelia. I promise I'm working, I just . . ."

"Need coffee?" Amelia asked, giving her a smile.

Stacey's eyes stayed wide. She'd always been intimidated by Amelia ever since she'd entered management.

"Yeah, just coffee. And maybe a donut," Stacey replied.

A moment passed where no one moved or said anything. That was when Amelia realized she and Daniel were blocking the door.

"Sorry. I'm in the way. You do what you need to."

Amelia went to move and bumped into Daniel *again*.

He reacted smoothly, stepping back and out of the way right after Amelia had gotten too close. They made it through the doorway with no coffee spilled, but by that time, they were lingering a little too close for comfort.

"Wow," Amelia said, laughing nervously. "I think I need to be away from people for a while. See you later!"

She turned and walked to her office without waiting for his reply. For a moment, she stared at her dark computer screen, feeling her cheeks burn in the aftermath of whatever the hell had just happened with Daniel.

Their usual conversations were short and to the point. He'd never *smiled* at her before. Then again, he'd never been unmarried before either.

Maybe he was happier single. He could have been like this with everyone by now, but she wouldn't know since they both kept their contact strictly professional.

Amelia knew she could turn this over in her head until she'd dissected every second of that interaction. She almost wanted to, just to see if remembering it would settle the subtle buzzing under her skin.

But she had work to do.

She powered on her computer to check her email. What she found was her corporate boss, Cheryl, telling her to remind everyone that no one was allowed to work from home under any circumstances.

Why not just do that themselves? Why did *her* name have to be on it?

She actually knew why, and she didn't like it. Amelia was the first point of contact when people had questions or complaints about policy, so it had to be her who sent it out. Judging by the fact that a few people worked from home when sick so they could save PTO, there were going to be issues with this reminder.

After she sent it out, she got exactly what she expected. She spent her whole morning sipping on coffee and responding to emails, which were mostly comprised of people asking different versions of the same question. *Can there be an exception to this ridiculous, no-exception rule?* By the time it was noon, Amelia was tired of having to deliver the bad news.

Luckily, her phone jingled, reminding her of lunch with her mom. They were discussing the annual family vacation and finishing off the last remaining to-do items before they left this weekend.

Her brother, John, lived in the city. But her parents preferred small-town life and lived about an hour away. Amelia didn't get to see them nearly as much as she wanted to. The vacation was a way for them to all reset and spend a week in each other's company.

She rubbed her eyes. She only had about fifteen minutes until she met with her mother, and she wanted to be in a decent mood. It took a lot to get her mom to drive to the city.

She stepped away from her computer, heading for the restaurant on the first floor of her office building, where she and her mom had agreed to meet.

Amelia was the spitting image of her mother, with the same dark hair, light brown eye color, and face shape. Her mom looked nice today. Her hair was curled and lay across her shoulders after a recent haircut. Her clothes were clean and complementary.

Amelia sighed in relief—her mom must have been in a good mental state.

"Hey, Mom," she said, giving her mother a hug.

"Hi, honey!" her mom replied brightly. "You look like you're exhausted. Is everything okay?"

"Everything's fine. I'm just busy, as always."

Her mom raised an eyebrow, but the hostess greeted them, stealing the opportunity to inquire further.

They sat, and the topic of food dominated their conversation up until they ordered. After their menus were gone and their drinks delivered, Amelia swirled her sweet tea, thankful for more caffeine.

"So, has anything big happened recently?"

"Nope," Amelia replied. "Just the usual work stuff. I'm trying to get everything squared away for next week. But honestly, I just think that everyone is looking forward to having me out of the office."

"I'm sure they all love you." Her mom gave her a smile. Amelia wasn't so sure, but she didn't say anything. "Any fun dates?"

Her stomach flipped. She should have seen this coming.

"Um, not really." She hoped the answer would make her mother drop it.

"Do you know Mr. Saylor's boy?"

Mr. Saylor lived next to her mom and dad, and while she liked her parents' neighbors, she didn't exactly *know* them.

"No, why?"

"Because his son is a doctor and he's looking for a vacation."

"And?"

"And I think you two would get along."

Amelia nearly choked on her drink. *"What?"*

"I'm setting you two up. I'm going to invite him on our trip so he can get to know you!"

Amelia leaned back in her chair. Her mom was a very determined woman, but this was too far. Setting her up on a week-long trip to the beach?

"Mom, no."

"Why not? What do you have to lose?"

"It's just weird," Amelia said, her anxiety making her sit up straighter. "I don't even know this guy."

"Yes, but you *could* know him."

"No way, Mom. No," she said firmly. She hoped this would be the end of it.

It wasn't.

"Give me one good reason why you can't let me invite someone on this trip. He can stay on the couch and you can finally test the waters with someone new!"

Amelia pursed her lips, desperately trying to think of a way out. That was when she saw Daniel walking to his car for lunch. Despite her predicament, her mind replayed their interaction from earlier.

Her mother followed Amelia's line of sight. "Who's that?"

"No one."

"I saw that look," she said. "Is that someone you have a *crush* on?"

"No." But Amelia's eyes drifted back to him, just in time to see him getting into a red Miata. That wasn't the car she'd pictured for him, yet she'd love to know *why* he'd gotten it. She'd love to know anything more about him.

"I think that's a yes, then."

Amelia blinked, forcing herself to look back at her mother. "What?"

"That man we just saw. He's *cute*, Amelia."

"Yes, he is," she said slowly, and her eyes returned to his car, where she watched him drive off. His soft compliment that morning flashed in her mind.

"What's that look for? Are you seeing him? Because if you are, I don't have to invite Mr. Saylor's boy on the trip."

Amelia only registered the last part of the sentence. "That would be *great*."

"And we can invite your new boyfriend instead."

Oh, *fuck*.

"N-no, Mom. He can't go."

"Why not?"

"He's busy, and we're not . . ."

"Dating?" Her mom raised her eyebrows. "With how you looked at him, I thought . . . Well, never mind. If you're not, I can still invite—"

"No need to invite him!" This would have been a great point to clear everything up. She wasn't dating Daniel, and she didn't want to be set up, but she knew that the latter point wasn't enough to convince her mom.

"So, you're dating him."

"Y-yes?" Her cheeks burned at the lie, but it was the only way she could get out of this. "But he's busy."

"You won't know until you ask," she said. "What's his name?"

"Daniel Anderson," Amelia muttered. She rubbed her forehead, unable to look at her mother. "Listen, Mom, I know you're excited, but I think we should just chill and talk ab— What are you doing?"

She was on her phone, lips curved into a smile. "Finding him on social media. I just sent him a friend request."

"What?"

"And when he accepts, I'm going to ask him myself. If you're dating someone, then I definitely want them to be invited on our trip."

This should have been where Amelia admitted she was lying. But now she was flustered. And she didn't do well when she was flustered.

"I'll . . . ask him myself."

"Great!" she said. "Oh, it says he works at the same company you do."

"Has he already accepted your friend request?"

"No. It's just on his profile. I can't stop looking at it. I'm just so *excited* you're dating again! What does he do at your company?"

She answered robotically as the horror of her situation dawned on her. "He's a director too."

"Oh, wow. That's so impressive for his age. Unless he's older."

Amelia had no clue how old he was.

"I'm not even sure," she said. Daniel couldn't be more than thirty-five, unless he was aging slowly.

"Oh, don't look so embarrassed. You know I'm not going to judge you as long as you're happy."

"I'm . . . I'm fine. Just thinking about how I'm going to ask him about the trip." Or tell him that her mother thought they were dating.

"Talking to your boyfriend shouldn't be stressful."

"It's just new," she said. "All of it is."

"Have you guys spent a night together?"

"Mom, are *you* okay? You seem really worried about this. More so than usual."

There could be many reasons for that. The main one being something that hadn't happened in a while.

A manic episode.

"Me?" she asked. "No, I'm fine, honey. I'm just excited for this trip. And worried about my only daughter."

Amelia nodded, but wondered if maybe her mom didn't realize it yet. Sometimes, this happened, and she didn't see it until later.

"All I ask is that you mention it to him. Or I will."

That made her focus snap back to the problem at hand. "I'll talk to him."

Daniel was probably going to laugh at her, or worse, report her to someone. He never talked about personal things at work, and he wasn't going to be happy that her mother had friend-requested him on Facebook.

But Amelia had done enough lying for the day. When she got back, she would tell Daniel exactly what had happened and deal with the consequences later.

CHAPTER TWO

DANIEL

"Hi, Daniel," Dana said, giving him a shy smile as she walked next to him in the hallway. "How are you?"

"I'm fine," he replied.

"I mean, how are you with . . . everything that's going on."

Ah. There it was. If there was one thing Daniel would erase, it was his coworkers' knowledge that his wife had left him. Ever since then, they had treated him as if he were a child, ready to explode at any moment. He was tired of it.

"Everything is good, just as usual."

He walked toward his office, leaving his employee behind, feeling the familiar tightness in his chest.

Yes, his wife left him.

Yes, he lived in an empty apartment with no one to share it with.

Yes, he was throwing himself into work in an attempt not to think about it, but he was fine. Work was fine. Everything was *fine*.

One day, even *he* would believe it.

After working for a few hours, Daniel left the office to get some lunch, needing to get away from his employees' stares and questions.

After he'd gotten food and sat at a table in the corner, his phone rang, and it was the last person he wanted to talk to.

"Hello?" Daniel answered, his voice level despite his annoyance.

"My boy! How are you?" Michael Anderson's booming voice said. Daniel hated that voice. It was the same one he used on TV while preaching to millions on his live streams. Once upon a time, Daniel wished his father would talk to him like a normal person, but now he knew he treated everything like a sermon, even family conversations.

"The same as always."

"Lucinda's been asking about you."

Daniel put down his fork, feeling a familiar rush of anger. "Good for her," he replied.

"We're both worried about your mental well-being," his father said. "I think you need to come down to the church. This is nothing God can't forgive."

Daniel rolled his eyes. He would rather be anywhere other than his father's church, which was nothing more than a TV studio and a not-for-profit moneymaking scheme that he ran. Daniel hadn't been religious in years.

"*I* didn't do anything. You committed adultery, with my wife, no less." The thought still made him sick, and he angrily pushed away his lunch.

"An affair due to neglect isn't an affair. Besides, I atoned for my sins."

Maybe with God, but certainly not with Daniel.

"Is this the reason why you called?" he asked, changing the subject.

"No, it's more important than that," his father started. "Lucinda and I have been talking. We want to go public with our relationship."

"What?"

Daniel had been enjoying this time where no one had known why his wife left. Despite their pity, it was easier this way. But once his father went public, Daniel knew he would say exactly how he met Lucinda.

And that was through him.

"Son, lying is a sin, and keeping my love for Lucinda secret is going to send us both to Hell. You don't want that, do you?"

"I don't want any of this. You can't tell people. This is going to ruin my life at work."

"God will take care of that."

Daniel gritted his teeth together. "You have to give me time, at least."

"I can do one more week."

"Thank you," Daniel said, feeling relieved. Usually, his father never gave him extra time. This felt almost like a gift.

"Anything for you, son," he said, as if he had actually done something for Daniel other than steal his wife. "Love you!" he added as he hung up.

Great, he had one week until his whole life was blown apart by his father, *again*. Daniel put his head in his hands and sighed.

What was he going to do? One of the very few things that had gone his way was that his father had kept Lucinda a secret for the four months they had been separated. Now, that was down the drain. His shame was going to be public, and there was nothing he could do about it.

People were never going to treat him normally ever again. Not while he was single, and not with this news coming out. How was he supposed to make it through the next week knowing that everyone was going to know his wife left him for his *father*?

After a moment, he knew he needed to get back to work. Maybe that would distract him from what was incoming. When he strode into his office, he was ready to answer emails and not think about anything to do with his personal life.

But that was when he saw Amelia Rogers sitting in one of the extra chairs.

She had the same pensive expression on her face that she always did, but it was set with a tenseness that was usually reserved for uncomfortable HR meetings. As far as he knew, Daniel hadn't done anything to warrant one.

"Hi, Daniel. Can we talk?" She gave him a tight smile. It was worlds different than the one he'd seen earlier in the day, when he'd been unable to resist the compliment she so deserved—despite her never seeming interested in talking to him.

He schooled his face as he sat at his desk.

His life wasn't blown apart *yet*, so he didn't need to act like it was.

"Yes, of course."

Amelia took a deep breath. "Have you checked your Facebook recently?"

His eyes widened, and he pulled out his phone. Daniel only used it to keep up with college friends, but his father was very active on the social media app. His heart raced as he looked at his notifications, but he only saw a friend request from a woman named Mandy Rogers.

"Well, now you have," Amelia said. "If you have a random request from a woman with the same last name as me, that's my mother."

"Your . . . mother?"

"Yes. Listen, there's no good way to break this, so I'll just say it." *Please don't say your mother knows my dad,* he silently begged.

"My mother thinks we're dating."

Daniel stared. That was the last thing he expected to hear, but it was far better than what he thought. "She . . . What? How?"

"It's a whole convoluted thing, but essentially, I was noticing you leaving the office while trying to get my mom not to set me up, and she made some assumptions."

"So, that's why she friend requested me? Is that all?"

"No. Unfortunately not. She *still* thinks we're dating and wants to invite you on our family trip. And I don't want to correct her because she insists on trying to set me up, even when I tell her no."

That was a lot to process. "Okay," he said slowly.

Amelia's face was redder than he'd ever seen it. "I know. I'm so sorry. My brain shut off, and I didn't know what to say."

"I can understand how that feels."

She winced, looking down at the hand that was fiddling with her sleeve. "I tried to say it was new and that you wouldn't be into it. Why would you want to go to a small, secluded beach island with people you barely know? I mean, the condo is already paid for, so it wouldn't cost you anything—"

A small beach island? Secluded?

"Where is it?"

"We go to Folly Beach every year. It's a way to unwind. We usually put away our phones to relax and enjoy the scenery. But you don't know us, and this is a ridiculous thing I've brought up, so I understand if you're totally judging me right now."

All he could think about was the idea of being on a small island, away from . . . *everyone*. That would be an excellent way to spend the next week before his father broke the news.

"Daniel?" Amelia asked. "Do I need to leave so you can report me to our boss?"

"No, it's not that big of a deal."

She let out a breath of relief. "Thank God."

"A beach vacation *would* be nice right now."

She huffed out a laugh. "Well, according to my mom, you're invited, but you'd have to date me, so . . ."

"When do you leave?"

She blinked. "W-what?"

"For the trip. When do you leave?"

"Saturday," she said. "Why do you ask?"

"And it's for a week?"

"Yes." She arched a brow. "Why?"

"I mean . . . She's invited me, and we *could* pretend to be together."

"W-what?"

"If you were okay with it, that is."

She stared at him for a long moment. "The better question is why are *you* okay with it?"

"Something is going to happen to me in a week. A vacation before this awful thing happens would be nice. And in turn, you would get your family off your back."

"But you don't take vacations."

"Which means I have a lot of PTO saved up. I think I can make it work—if I'm invited, that is."

"But you'll be *dating* me."

"I think the better term is *fake* dating."

"Semantics." She waved her hand in the air. "The point is—this is wild. For both of us to do." She hesitated for a moment. "So, you're really considering doing this?"

"I am. Unless that's not what you were getting at."

"Are you kidding?" Amelia leaned forward. "Because I can't tell. My mom will have the time of her life if I bring my boyfriend with me. Fake boyfriend, I mean. But even *fake* boyfriends have to do certain things. Like hold hands. Share a bed."

"Would your parents let us share a bed if we're not married?"

"Of course, they're not from the 1960s. They know how couples work."

Sharing a bed. Sure. He could do that. "Then sharing a bed would be fine."

"But *still*." She waved a hand again. "Even if I can convince my brother to give us the room with the adjoined bathroom, we'd still be with my family."

"There are bedrooms?"

"We rent a waterfront condo. It's right on the beach and has plenty of room for us all. We're not all staying in one room. That would be . . ." She shuddered. "Also, people here might have some questions if you're leaving the same week I am. And my mom might post on Facebook, which I bet someone will hunt down because they always are gossiping about *something*."

As she spoke, Daniel noticed that she never seemed to sit still. Having a conversation felt like he was watching a performance.

"And they'd definitely figure out we were together," he finished for her.

"Exactly. And that's why it's a bad idea, so we can forget about it and pretend this never happened."

"No, it's a great idea."

"Huh?"

"I need people here to think I've moved on from my ex-wife."

"You do? Why?"

"She's with someone else. Someone . . . well-known."

Amelia raised her eyebrows, and he expected her to question him. "Is this the news that drops in a week?"

"It is."

"And you want to look like you've moved on." Her hands moved as if she were drawing a graph. It somehow helped him make sense of this strange situation.

"Exactly."

"So . . . What, we pretend here too?"

"For a short amount of time. Then we break up."

"Wow, okay." She leaned back in her chair. "This is not how I expected this conversation to go."

"Me either. Is this something that you would be willing to do?"

"I think so, but there're a lot of logistics we need to work out. Especially since we leave in two days. How about we go to dinner tonight and I can tell you more about it?" she offered.

Their conversations about not work-related things, coupled with their possible fake relationship, had thrown them into new territory. Dinner with her would push them beyond that.

But he couldn't remember a time when he went out to dinner with a woman who wasn't Lucinda, and the idea of it, especially since it was Amelia, made his heart skip a beat.

"Sounds good," Daniel said. "What time do you get off?"

"I try to leave at five."

He had been staying late, trying not to think about his life, but he could leave at five if he wanted to. "Okay, I can leave then. Any ideas for a restaurant?"

"The Metro Café Diner is close by."

He had only been there once, and it was back in college. It was a casual breakfast spot, which was more than okay with him. He didn't think his flustered mind could handle somewhere fancy. Then he would have an even harder time not thinking of this as a date.

"Sure," he replied. "I'll see you tonight."

Amelia nodded at him, giving him a small smile as she stood to leave. And that was when Daniel saw the curve of her hips. He hadn't looked at a woman since he and Lucinda had dated. But now he was single, and he felt like a kid in high school looking at a girl for the first time.

He only let his eyes linger for a second, and then he tore them away. She walked out of his office soon after.

Daniel's mind was a jumbled mess, and he did what he usually did when he felt this way. He called his sister.

Terri was older than him, and they had been very close all their lives. She and her wife, Chrissy, had been blissfully living in Nashville for the last five years, and recently, they adopted a little boy named Tommy. However, since their father had been told by God that being gay was a sin, Terri hadn't talked to him since she came out in high school.

"You will never guess what I am about to do," Daniel told her.

"Murder our father," Terri said, her voice level.

"Maybe soon, but I think I'm going to pretend to be a coworker's boyfriend."

There was silence on the line and then a laugh. "No way."

"I'm serious. She asked me to."

"Why?"

"Something about a lie she told her mom. I'm not too sure of the details, but Dad is going public with Lucinda."

"Wait, seriously?"

"Yes, and if I can have a pretend girlfriend, it'll make life so much easier for me at the office."

"And why's that?"

"Because it'll look like I have moved on."

"Okay . . . I'm kind of following now. So, why tell me this?"

His fingers trailed over his desk nervously. "I think this is the wildest thing I've ever done. Are you about to convince me out of it?"

"I mean . . . Honestly, this isn't any worse than what our father did. What's this woman's name?"

"Amelia Rogers."

"A . . . meeeelia Rog-erssss."

"Are you looking her up?"

"Of course." There was a pause. "Oh, hey, she's really hot."

"Terri, you're married."

"But we can still appreciate other people. It's like art, and this woman is definitely something. Does she look as good in person as she does in photos?"

"Better," he said, his voice low. He hadn't even seen her in any photos, but he simply knew the answer was yes, judging by the way he'd stared at her as she was leaving the office.

"Cute. You've even noticed how pretty she is. When would you start this whole charade?"

"Saturday."

"Wait, why Saturday?"

"Because I would also be going on her family vacation as her fake boyfriend."

"Am I being pranked right now?" Terri asked. "There is no way you would say yes to something like that."

"I do need a vacation, Terri."

"I mean, yes, you do, but seriously? You're going on vacation with this woman?"

"That was part of the deal," he explained. "I help her out and she helps me out."

"How long will you be gone?"

"A week."

"*A week?* You couldn't even spend a week with your wife, much less a stranger."

"So, I shouldn't do it, right?"

"I'm not saying that . . ."

"Then, what are you saying?" Frustration seeped into his voice.

"I'm saying that this is *so* out of character for you. Now, me? Five years ago? Yeah, I would have pulled a stunt like this, but not you."

"I know this is out of character, but Dad is about to drop a serious bomb on my life. I don't want pity, Terri."

"I know you don't," she said sympathetically. "And I'm not against the idea, but I also seriously doubt you're the kind of person who can spend a week with some random woman."

"I know I'm not, but as far as I know, Amelia is reasonable. We're going to dinner tonight to talk more details."

"Okay, that's a good sign," she said. "Hopefully, you can learn a little more about her. If you get any . . . Lucinda-type vibes from her, then don't go."

"So, you're saying I should do it?"

"I think you should try it. Maybe doing something out of character is exactly what you need right now."

"That's what it feels like."

"Then take a risk. Be a little more like your older sister."

"Didn't you get stuck with a truck driver in Montana?"

"Yes, but I also met Chrissy there."

Daniel rolled his eyes, but he couldn't help the glimmer of hope that he felt. Maybe this stunt would help him find the happiness and stability that Terri had.

"Okay, then I'll go to this dinner and see how I feel."

"Keep me posted about it."

"Also, don't tell Mom."

"I would never. She would kill you. Oh, Tommy, honey, Play-Doh *doesn't* go in your—Daniel, I have to go. I'll talk to you later."

Daniel laughed and said his goodbyes to his sister. After he got off the phone, he wondered what the dinner would bring. Maybe Amelia would have some sort of red flag he could catch before it all started.

Or maybe she didn't, and he would get to go on a vacation after all.

CHAPTER THREE

AMELIA

With Metro Café's bright lights and loud music, Amelia wouldn't call it a first choice for a date. Not that this was one.

She figured something more casual would be better for her and Daniel. She didn't know what it was called when two people were discussing fake dating, but it certainly wasn't fancy-dinner worthy.

The two of them walked in around five-thirty. The cafe was usually its busiest at breakfast, so it was empty when they arrived. A bored-looking hostess led them to a table near a window.

Daniel was as aloof as ever, and now that Amelia had a few hours to think on it, she had a few concerns.

The main one being how they had only ever interacted as coworkers. Her family would see right through them if that continued. When she was with Andrew, they had been all over each other, and if she and Daniel couldn't at least walk close together, her family would immediately tell her she was with the wrong guy.

"Amelia?"

She blinked out of her thoughts. Both Daniel and the waitress were looking at her expectantly. "What?"

"Sorry, she's had a rough day at work," he explained with a smile she had never seen before. Wide and bright, it was so different from the small one she had seen earlier that day. It radiated charisma. "What are you having to drink?"

Amelia inwardly screamed. Did she seriously just zone out so bad that she didn't even notice their waitress? Andrew would've yelled at her for a mistake like that.

"Um, water, please," she said and waited for the waitress to walk off before adding, "I promise I'm not usually rude to waitstaff."

"I know," Daniel said. "If memory serves, you gave a $50 tip out of your own pocket to a pizza delivery driver. It was talked about so much that even *I* heard it."

"When was that?"

Daniel shrugged. "Like a year ago? It's one of the very few things I know about you."

She was surprised he knew anything about her at all.

"I don't even remember it, but it's something I'd do."

They lapsed into silence and she busied herself with looking at the menu. The waitress came back, and they both ordered breakfast platters, despite the fact that it was evening.

"So, tell me about this trip," Daniel said, looking at her. "And about your family."

"Right." Time to get down to business. "So, my family has a tradition of going to the beach every year. My parents live about an hour away from here, so we don't get to hang out all the time, especially since I was promoted to director."

Daniel nodded, lips pressed together. The hours they both pulled were long, and Amelia wondered if his had anything to do with his failed marriage.

Nope. No. She wasn't going to be asking questions about *that*. It was none of her business.

"Anyway, we're going to Folly Beach."

Daniel nodded. "You said that. It seems very relaxing."

"My dad knows an owner of a condo there that can fit my whole family. So, each year, we go to try to get some family time. Fair warning, my dad is going to want to pay for food. I mean, unless your wife took all your money, I'm sure your salary is enough to cover that, but . . ." She stopped, realizing what she was saying.

Daniel was still only looking at her. He didn't look mad, but he also didn't look happy.

"I am so sorry," she apologized. "I need to stop talking before I say more stupid things."

"I'm not offended."

"Really?"

"In fact, the opposite. I'm very tired of people treating me as if I'm going to break at any time."

Amelia nodded. She could understand that. She blew out a relieved breath.

"But no, I am very fortunate that I don't have to pay my ex-wife alimony." His lips pressed together, as if the reason why he didn't have to pay alimony wasn't a good one. "I can pay for my own food."

"I can too, but my parents are incredibly stubborn. Plus, you're the first guy I've let them meet in five years, so be prepared for special treatment. If you go through with this, that is."

"None of your exes made the cut?"

"No, it's not that. I just haven't dated in five years."

"How come?" he asked. Amelia raised her eyebrows, not expecting it to be a topic of conversation. He noticed, and his cheeks turned slightly pink. "I mean . . . you've obviously had options."

"What does that mean?" she asked, tilting her head to one side.

"I . . . I don't know if I should elaborate."

"Come on, I'm your fake girlfriend. I won't judge."

"You should probably not use the word *fake* if you're referring to me."

"Fine. I'm your *girlfriend*. Now, tell me what you meant."

"I meant . . . you're beautiful, Amelia. Any man would be lucky to have you."

Her skin grew warm at the words. Daniel was far better at wooing than she thought. He must have barely had to try with Lucinda.

"Was that too far?" he asked. "Should I take it back?"

"No. But you should save that for when we're at the beach." She couldn't help the smile that turned her lips upward. "And to answer your question, my last relationship . . . didn't end so well."

"I'm sorry to hear that."

"It's fine. It's in the past. My mom thinks I should get back out there, but I'm really fine being on my own."

"I feel the same way. About the divorce."

"Really?"

"Yes. I'm fine."

"Then we're just two fine people pretending to date. Easy, right?"

"I don't think anything about this is going to be easy," he said. "I don't . . . I haven't dated in a long time."

"Me either, but it can't be *that* hard. We just hold hands and casually touch. It's not like we need to fuck or anything."

Daniel's eyes widened.

"Sorry," she said, holding up her hands. "I sometimes don't have a filter. Especially after a day at the office. I can keep it in check, I promise."

"It's fine. Just unexpected. And if this is who you are outside of the office, then I should probably see it." He gave her another smile, just like the one he'd given the waitress.

Amelia could remember when Andrew barely used to huff out a laugh at her little quirks. He soon didn't think it was funny at all.

But she and Daniel were only doing this for a few weeks. Maybe two. Hopefully, she wouldn't get on his nerves in that time.

"You're right. But if you're ever uncomfortable, or it's too much—" Or if *she* was too much. "—then let me know."

Daniel's dark eyes were back on her again. By the way his jaw went slack, she wondered if he had ever been told this in his life.

"That's helpful," he said. "Thank you."

"I'm just doing the right thing. I'm not comfortable if you're not comfortable. Let me know if we're ever going too far."

"I will."

"And once again, I'm sorry if I'm being weird. Today was a lot."

"Fake-dating discussions aside, I saw you sent out a controversial email."

"It wasn't my idea, that's for sure. No one was abusing the work-from-home policy. Our executives just want people in the office."

"It's an unfair rule," he said. "If we treat our employees like people, then they'll have an easier time doing the work."

"I agree." She gave him a mock toast with her drink. "It's going to be so nice getting away for a bit."

"Absolutely. I haven't been to the beach in a very long time."

"Was the last time your honeymoon?" After she said it, she cringed. *Why* did she bring up his marriage? The first rule of dating, fake or not, was not to bring up the ex. "Where did you go?"

"Hawaii. Lucinda spent most of the time posing for Instagram shots. I hear those photos got a lot of likes."

"Did . . . you enjoy that?"

"Does it matter?"

"I think it does." Amelia was dying to know more, yet the pinched expression on his face made her question if she should even ask.

"You and Lucinda would disagree there then," he said.

That was far sadder than she expected.

"You know what? Fuck the ex. We're talking about the *future* now."

"Okay, let's talk about the future."

"It's all sunny beaches from here. And a lot of walking. We like to pretty much park the car for a week unless we find a restaurant a little farther away we want to go to."

"Sounds like exactly what I need."

They were interrupted by their food's arrival, and Amelia's stomach panged with hunger. She tore into her pancakes, forgetting about the man across from her. After half of them were gone, she looked up.

Daniel was cutting his neatly. She wondered if he'd watched her in horror as she stuffed the food in her mouth.

Be normal. She desperately needed to be normal.

She paused to look for something to entertain her. What she settled on was him. Daniel ate slowly and methodically, just like he seemed to do his work. She knew she was straight chaos, but she'd have to tone it down for him.

"Are you already finished?"

She blinked, realizing she hadn't eaten in a good few moments. "No," she said. "Just taking a minute."

She resumed, but slower this time. After she'd almost finished her plate, she looked back up at him.

"So," she started, "do you think that this could work?"

Even after she shoveled her food into her mouth like a gremlin?

"I think it could."

"Great." She felt relieved. She hadn't blown this just yet. "Maybe after this, my mom will get off my back about being in a relationship."

"Being single isn't a problem. Sometimes, it's better this way."

"Right? I was relieved when Andrew left."

"I felt the same way with Lucinda."

Amelia wondered if he had dealt with the same things she had. Did Lucinda put him down at any chance she got? Did she get angry and take it out on him? She wouldn't wish that on her worst enemy.

A cold bed and silent home were small prices to pay for not being put through that again. All she needed was her work and her family. That was it.

Her mother didn't understand. She thought Amelia was lonely and needed a partner. But she didn't *need* one because she didn't need the inevitable fighting that came with it.

She was fine. And pretending was easier than trying to get others to understand.

CHAPTER FOUR

DANIEL

As Daniel put in his PTO request, he couldn't help but think of just how well the dinner went. Amelia was honest, discussing things with him directly rather than beating around the bush. Her smiles took over her whole face and felt far more genuine than Lucinda's ever had.

And now that he had a better understanding of what kind of person Amelia was, he felt better about his impromptu plans. He was *excited* for them, even.

He glanced at his watch. He'd gone back to the office after dinner to get a few more emails answered and to request the time off. It was eight when he finally acknowledged he had to leave, and he was hoping it was late enough that he could fall asleep without his mind keeping him awake.

However, Daniel knew he wouldn't be getting any rest the moment he walked through the door. Lucinda's perfume wafted through the entryway, as if she had sprayed it just moments before.

She lounged on the couch, acting like she still lived there. She had meticulously dyed light ash blonde hair that showed no hints of her natural dark color. She kept it cut in a sharp bob that stopped right at her jawline, a new style she'd kept ever since she found herself with an older man. Her gray eyes had always been piercing, and now, they were focused on him as he walked into the living room.

"What are you doing here?" he asked, his voice tight. He hadn't seen her since their divorce, and it hurt to be in the same room.

"I just came to see how you were doing with the news," she said airily, even though it always carried a sharp edge. "I know Michael called you today."

"He did, but you shouldn't be here. Does your new *boyfriend* know?"

Lucinda smiled. "Of course he does. He just wants to make sure you're okay."

"Yes, because the man who stole my wife from me definitely cares about my well-being."

"You let me go," she reminded, her smile fading. "This was on you, not me."

"You cheated."

"You left."

"No, I didn't."

"Emotionally, you did. You never cared about me in the way I needed. So I found someone who did."

Daniel sighed. They had been through this a million times over. It was opening wounds that hadn't truly healed. "I tried, Lucinda, but I'll never be what you want me to be."

He could remember when all he strived for was to be what Lucinda wanted. He worked so they had money. He got promoted even though his heart wasn't in it.

It was exhausting.

But it was never enough. There was always someone with more money, with an easier job, and she had no problem with reminding him of that fact.

If it wasn't the money, then there was someone more emotionally available. There was someone better looking or someone who looked at her the right way.

She was chasing a dream, and he'd spent far too long killing himself to keep up with her.

"You didn't try hard enough. And now, I'm gone," Lucinda said. It was meant to stab him. But he didn't love her anymore. He didn't miss her or want her back.

He *wanted* her gone.

"Why did you really come here?" he asked flatly. "Was it just to rub it in?"

Lucinda smiled again. That was exactly what she was doing. Daniel wasn't really in the mood for this. He was never in the mood for Lucinda's mind games.

He couldn't believe that he once loved her. There was a time when he thought her words were a sign of how smart she was, and he had fallen for it and married her. Now that he was on the opposite end of that marriage, he looked at it as if it had been one of the worst mistakes of his life.

"And how have you been?" she asked, walking around the empty apartment. "You haven't even decorated."

"I haven't had the time to."

Lucinda rolled her eyes. "Of course. Your job is *so* important."

That had been another point of contention—how late Daniel worked.

"You wanted me to make money," he reminded her.

"Not like this. Haven't you ever heard of passive income?"

It was his turn to roll his eyes. "That's not how it works."

"And the apartment, you're never here. Why didn't you let me have it?"

"You're living in my father's mansion," Daniel said. "You don't need it. Unless you plan on cheating on him too."

She laughed and shook her head, but he knew that she could never focus on one person. There was always someone better out there.

He knew he should care about his father enough to warn him. He knew that there had to be some form of loyalty that he could call on in order to tell his father what Lucinda would probably do.

But he didn't care. Not really. Daniel doubted he would ever call his father at all, much less to tell him what his ex-wife might do.

"You're never going to be happy," she said. "Not without me."

She turned and walked away. Daniel felt his fists clench, until he realized that he would be away for a week where she couldn't find him. That thought alone was enough to calm him down. He ignored the way she swayed her hips as she walked toward the door, as if inviting him to see what he was missing out on. But it didn't work. He felt nothing, and because he hadn't loved her in so long, he couldn't remember why he ever did.

He rolled his eyes again as she shut the door. He couldn't wait for vacation.

CHAPTER FIVE

AMELIA

Her mom had said that she was waiting for an answer, but Amelia knew she wouldn't wait forever. As soon as Daniel told her he had the time off the following morning, she texted the family's group chat.

The reaction was instantaneous.

Amelia: Daniel said he would like to join us.

John: Who the fuck is Daniel?

Amelia: My boyfriend.

John: EXCUSE ME? Since when are you dating?

Mom: Yay! I'm so glad he could join us!

There was no going back now, Amelia realized. Her nerves were frayed from lying to her family, and she knew they were going to be talking about this all day. John knew of her aversion to dating since he had one of his own, but she didn't know if he'd see right through the lie or not.

Despite the stress, she still needed to get to work, so she put down her phone and ignored any new messages until she got on the MARTA.

John: Hold on, Mom. You knew?

Mom: Of course! She just told me yesterday.

John: What is even happening right now?

Amelia: We're going on vacation and Mom invited my boyfriend. That's what happened.

John: Wait, so there's five of us total? How are we going to get there? I refuse to all squish in the back of Mom's car.

He was right. Their mom's car *could* fit five people, but not comfortably. Amelia really didn't want to be squished between Daniel and her brother for five hours.

Amelia: I'll take my car.

John: HA. Yeah right. You hate driving.

Amelia: I'm not asking Daniel to drive. He moved his entire schedule around to come. I'll be fine.

Mom: Are you sure, honey?

Dad: We could rent a car.

Amelia smiled at her dad's text. Her dad was smart and resourceful, but even with a bigger car, she didn't want to throw Daniel to the wolves this early, especially with no escape route available.

Maybe *she* didn't want to be thrown to the wolves, either.

Amelia: No, it would be a nightmare to get a rental so quickly. I'll drive. It'll be fine, guys.

Mom: Okay, but only if you're sure.

Dad: Amelia is very capable of taking care of herself. Just call us if you need anything, okay?

Amelia: Always.

She smiled and put away her phone. It took until she was in her office to realize what she had offered to do.

Amelia hated driving; John wasn't wrong about that. It made her anxiety rise just thinking about it. She only had a car, so she could drive herself and John to her family's house for holidays. She didn't even use it to get to work.

But it wasn't like she had a better option. She really didn't want to spend any amount of time in the back seat of a cramped car with three people.

It would be better to be in the driver's seat with one person, even if she barely knew him.

At least it wasn't the man her mom was trying to set her up with.

Amelia then realized she was staring at a wall and being entirely unproductive. So, she attempted to focus on her work, which essentially meant approving or denying HR issues and escalations. She was done by five, and then she turned on her out-of-office message and shut down her computer.

Sighing, she rubbed her eyes for a moment and then stood to leave. She wondered if she should text Daniel to make plans for the next day, but she ran right into him as she left her office.

Quite literally.

She was met with a solid chest and the smell of pine and cedar. He was warm in the cool air of the office, and she was tempted to stay and savor the heat he provided.

But she stepped back, rubbing her cheek from where it had been pressed against his shirt.

"Sorry," Daniel said. "I was just about to knock."

Amelia took in his appearance. He had his work laptop in hand and a backpack slung over his shoulder.

"Are you leaving already?" she asked.

"Yes. I finished early."

"Wow, that's great. You normally stay later."

"I was hoping to catch you before you left. We still need to figure out the plan for tomorrow, right?"

"Right." She nodded. "*We* have to plan things. Usually my brother and dad do all the thinking."

"How about you tell me what you have and I'll do some of it as well."

"Sure," she said, motioning for him to follow her to the elevator.

"I looked it up last night. It's about five hours from here."

"Yep. We usually leave around ten in the morning to get there at three. In past years, I'd get up earlier and drive to their house, but we aren't doing that this year."

"Why not?"

They walked into the elevator, and Amelia opened her mouth to respond, but someone else ran in before she could speak.

Andrea looked between the two of them. "You're both leaving early."

"We have big plans," Amelia said. She glanced at Daniel, hoping she hadn't just said the wrong thing, but he gave her a tiny nod.

"Wait, both of you?"

"We're going to the beach," was Daniel's simple yet telling answer.

"At the same time?"

"Yes."

"To the same beach?"

"Yep," Daniel said. Andrea turned to look at both of them, and her eyes went back and forth between them for a long second, as if trying to picture them together. Amelia didn't blame her—she was trying to picture the same thing.

The elevator door opened, and they were all spared any more awkwardness.

"Um, have fun, then!" Andrea said, and she raced to her car. Amelia wondered how long it was going to take for the entire office to know.

"That's going to be a talking point for the whole week."

"Unfortunately," she muttered under her breath. Judging by what she'd heard Andrea and Dana say only the day before, she knew it wasn't all going to be good talk.

"What were you saying before Andrea joined us in the elevator?"

"Oh, right. We're not going to my parents' house because we're driving by ourselves. I figured the two of us being alone in a car together is better than all five of us being in a tiny car."

"That's a good idea."

"If one of us isn't dead in a ditch by the time we hit the South Carolina line, we should be fine for a week."

Daniel chuckled. "Hopefully. I'll text you my address."

She nodded and expected him to leave. But then he glanced over at Andrea's car, which was still in the parking lot.

"Do you still want to pretend to date here at work?" she asked.

"I do."

"Andrea is still in her car, and I'm pretty sure she's watching. We could, I don't know, hug? Maybe?"

Daniel gave her a sideways glance, and she had a split second to wonder if it had been a good idea to suggest this at all. But then he wrapped his long arm around her shoulder, pulling her into a tight hug. Amelia felt her entire face almost explode in heat as she let it happen.

He smelled too good. His body was too warm, and she could easily get addicted to this if she let herself.

"There," he said, pulling away. "That will make tomorrow easier."

"Right," she said, feeling her heart race. *Easier.*

CHAPTER SIX

DANIEL

Daniel was no stranger to pretending; unfortunately, over the last many years, he'd become very good at it. Lucinda had shown him exactly how to do it by instructing him how to smile, how to act, how to move around her. He wasn't allowed to be himself. He couldn't stray from her side, much less tire or get a moment alone, lest she lash out at him.

It had been tough work following her instructions the best he could, and even though it had been months since their divorce, his tank was still near empty. And that worried him for the impending vacation with Amelia and her family.

Could he just be *himself*, or would she expect him to be and act a certain way? As he waited for her to pick him up the next morning, the panic set in—was this going to be relaxing at all? Amelia seemed far nicer than Lucinda, much less high-maintenance, but all of that could change the second the pressure to perform fell on them both.

She arrived a few minutes late. Daniel was waiting in the lobby of his building and watched her pull up in a gray Honda CR-V. She had on a tank top, looking more casual than he had ever seen her.

He had a hard time not staring at her exposed arms. Seeing her in anything other than her usual work attire made his stomach flip. This was a side to her no one else at work had seen.

Amelia smiled when she saw him. He put his suitcase in the rear cargo area right next to her smaller one and climbed into the front passenger seat. The AC was lightly blowing, and she had soft, melodic music playing. Her car was perfect for two people on a trip, much better than the Miata Lucinda had insisted he buy.

She yawned. "I didn't get any sleep last night."

"Why don't we stop for coffee?" he offered.

"I don't want to add too much time to the drive," she replied.

"I'd rather you have what you need than be miserable driving. Go ahead and stop."

"Thank you." Her voice sounded relieved. "I was worried you'd be the kind of person that wants to drive straight there and never stop."

When they got to the Starbucks drive-through, she ordered him a tea and paid for it without a second glance in his direction. Usually, Lucinda made a scene of making him pay for everything.

Amelia pulled out of the parking lot and merged onto the interstate. They rode in silence for a while, and Daniel wondered if he should do something to fill the void. Lucinda always nagged him about that.

"So . . ." Amelia started. "Are you excited for a vacation with a family you don't know?"

"Uh . . . kind of," he said. "I'm a little nervous, actually."

"You don't have to worry. My mom can be a lot, but she's really nice, and my dad is too."

"I don't have a good track record with fathers." He remembered how Lucinda's dad had threatened him with a shotgun when they first started dating. Every time he saw him after that, her father glared at Daniel as if daring him to step out of line.

"My dad's really relaxed," Amelia said. "I don't think you could do anything to upset him, except maybe murder someone."

"In my experience, dads are really weird around their daughter's boyfriends."

She scoffed. "You mean the shovel talk thing? Oh no, he'd never. And if he does, let me know, and I'll have a word with him."

"What would you say?"

"That I'm capable of making my own life choices and handling the fallout if it comes to that. But I seriously doubt he's going to say anything. He's never before. My mom might ask questions, so we should probably agree on a story."

"What will she ask?"

"Probably everything to know about us as a couple. She gets in these moods where she wants to fix things. She was in one the other day."

"Then what is our story?" he asked.

"Something simple. I asked you out a few weeks ago and we've been dating ever since."

"*You* asked *me* out?"

"Can't a woman ask a guy out these days?"

"They can. I've just . . . My wife was old-fashioned."

"Are *you* old-fashioned?"

"I don't know what I am. I just went along with what she wanted."

"That's no way to fake date." She took a sip of her coffee. "The best way is for *both* people to do a little of what they want. That way, they both have fun."

"Seems simple," he said. "What about your brother?"

"My brother's name is John and he's . . . I don't really know how to describe him, actually."

"Really?"

"He's . . . different, but in a good way. He usually uses these trips to meet new people and go do his own thing. He's also really relaxed."

All of it sounded too perfect, as if no one was going to fight on the trip. In his world, something always went wrong on vacation. And usually, it ended with massive arguments.

"All you need to do is sit there and look hot and we should be good," Amelia said. "We're breaking up after a few weeks of this, so it doesn't have to be perfect."

Daniel was a perfectionist at heart, so he knew this was going to be a challenge, no matter how simple it seemed. "Sit there and look hot. Got it."

"I mean, also, maybe talk to them. Like, don't just actually sit there and do nothing."

"I figured I would talk too."

Amelia chuckled, but it turned into a sigh. Her nervousness was obvious, and who could blame her? This thing they were attempting to do was incredibly outside the box.

They made small talk up until they were halfway into South Carolina, but she got quiet and seemed to focus more on the road. Daniel wasn't offended. He'd rather her focus than get in a wreck, but he figured maybe she was tiring out. After all, she had been driving for hours. Maybe he needed to offer to take over for a bit.

He then saw brake lights ahead of them, and though Amelia's eyes were on the road, the cars were stopping way too fast. So much so that he knew they were going to hit someone.

"Shit!" Amelia slammed on the brakes. She was as fast as she possibly could have been, but there was no way a human could have stopped in time. The CR-V nosedived, and at the last second, she managed to pull to the shoulder to avoid hitting them.

The car that had been behind theirs slammed into the one that had stopped so suddenly, and the bumper of the car that had been behind them flew off.

Silence enveloped the interior of the car and Daniel looked at Amelia. Her lips were pressed together in a fine line, and she gripped the wheel so tightly her knuckles were white.

She climbed out without a word. Daniel grabbed the keys and climbed out too. He could hear the people involved in the crash yelling about who caused the accident, but he couldn't care less about that. He followed Amelia, who had gone far into the grass of the nearby field.

"Are you okay?" he asked, the words sounding inadequate after what had happened.

"I'm fine," she said, but her voice shook.

"That was a smart move, pulling over to the shoulder like that."

"I should have seen it sooner. We haven't even made it to the beach, and I've already caused a problem."

"What problem did *you* cause?" he asked.

She gestured around them.

"Amelia, that really wasn't your fault."

"You're probably right, but I'm just so . . ." She ran her hands through her hair, shutting her eyes tightly. "I'm fine. I'm totally fine."

Daniel wasn't so sure. "What if I drove for a bit?"

"I can't ask you to do that."

"I'm offering. You're shaken up after that, and rightfully so."

"But . . ."

"I really don't mind."

"I'm an *adult*," she snapped. "I should be able to drive for a few hours."

"You're not a bad driver, and this wasn't your fault. I only want to help."

Her shoulders sank. She looked back at the car and sighed. "Fine. You can drive. I hate driving anyway."

"You hate driving?" he asked. "And you drove this far?"

"It makes me so nervous. For this reason exactly." She gestured to the accident again. Police had arrived and were taking statements. Both drivers were still yelling at each other.

"You saved us from being involved in that," he said. "Let's tell the police what we saw and then get back on the road."

"Okay. Let me give you my keys." Her hands brushed over her pockets, but they didn't find anything. "Wha—where did I . . ."

"I have them."

"Did I leave them in the car?" She groaned. "I hate it when shit like this happens. I start making so many stupid mistakes when I'm flustered."

"It's fine," Daniel assured her, and when her eyes turned to him, he could see that she didn't believe him. "It really is. Now, let's go tell the police what we saw."

After they gave their statements, they were free to go. Daniel climbed into the driver's seat of the car. Amelia was quiet when she got in. They pulled back onto the road, and he focused on ensuring they were far enough away from other people.

But only a few minutes into the drive, he heard her stomach rumble. "Are you hungry?" he asked.

"What? No. I'm fine."

"Do we need to stop?"

"No, I'm good! I can skip lunch."

"So you *are* hungry."

"I don't want to keep stopping for something so small."

Amelia's hunger wasn't small to him, but he had a feeling he wouldn't be able to convince her of that. She was stubborn, but not in the ways he was used to. It seemed she was insistent on *not* taking care of herself, *not* inconveniencing others.

"Would it help if I said I was hungry too?"

"Maybe. Are you?"

"I am. How about we just get something really quick?"

"Okay," she said slowly. "That works for me."

Daniel found a Taco Bell and pulled into a parking spot. This time, he paid for their food, even as she tried to hand him her card.

"You got the coffee. I got the food."

Amelia huffed and put away her card. "Fine. If you insist."

They found a table in the corner and sat to eat. Amelia tore into her food much like she had at the diner. She must have been starving. She was finished far before he was, but most of his time was spent figuring out how not to make a mess of the burrito he'd ordered.

"Okay," she admitted, the stress gone from her voice. "Maybe I was hungry."

"I'm glad it helped."

"I always wind up at Taco Bell when I'm on vacation."

"Really?"

"Yeah. One time, John had a meltdown in the car, and I mean a crying, screaming meltdown. We had to stop and get food because he's such a baby when he's hungry. It was this exact one, actually."

"My sister's like that."

"Luckily, I don't do all of those things, but I just get anxious. And sometimes cranky. Sorry you had to see that."

"If that's what you're like when you almost get into a car crash while hungry, then I'd say you have a pretty level head."

"I promise I usually don't let myself get that hungry. Or into car crashes. I can usually stick to a routine, but vacations always mess me up."

"I'll remind you to eat," he said. "That way, you don't have to worry about it too much."

"And maybe I won't inhale it. I know it's not the most ladylike thing ever."

He shrugged. Her eating style didn't bother him. "I figured you were hungry."

"I'm also just a fast eater. I used to race my dad when I was a kid."

Daniel couldn't help but smile. It seemed like she had the kind of father she could do those things with. He only wished he did too.

He made quick work of his burrito, not wanting to keep her waiting for too long. By the time he was done, she was standing and ready to go.

"Are you still okay with driving?"

"Yeah," he said, relieved he could help in some way. "I really don't mind."

"Thank God. The last thing I want to do is be behind the wheel right now."

CHAPTER SEVEN

AMELIA

It started to feel like a vacation after she gave up the wheel to Daniel. Her family had been right. She wasn't good with driving, not in the slightest. Thankfully, he seemed to be able to handle it well enough that she wasn't worried about letting him drive her car.

As they drove, she occasionally told him about certain sights or things to do, especially as they made their way through Charleston. They pulled into Folly Beach in the midafternoon, making good time despite the traffic and the earlier holdup with the accident.

Her family had just arrived too, and they were parked in one of the extra spaces, unloading the car. The condominium was right on the beach, next to the town center. In the summer, it was a busy area. Her parents joked that this was the busiest place they liked to be.

"That's them," she said, pointing to their car.

Daniel nodded and pulled up beside them. He took a deep breath, looking like he was preparing to go on stage at a show.

"Are you okay?"

"Just . . . getting ready to be a fake boyfriend."

Before she could ask him what he meant, she heard her mother calling her name. She got out of the car and had only a moment to appreciate the windy, salty air before she was pulled into a tight hug.

Soon after, Daniel was in one too. He looked very uncomfortable for all of one moment before his face broke out into the same smile he had given the waitress back in the diner. Amelia blinked, still unused to seeing this side of him.

"It's so nice to meet you! I'm Mandy," her mom said, pulling away so she could better admire him. "You're so handsome."

Amelia expected him to awkwardly laugh or even ignore the compliment. That's what she would have done.

"Thank you. I can see where Amelia gets her beauty from."

She stared, trying to piece together the man she had just spent the car ride with and the man that was talking to her mother. She then remembered how he looked in the car. He had been preparing himself for this.

He knew exactly how to fake a relationship.

"Nice to meet you, son." Her dad, Randy, walked up to shake Daniel's hand. "Glad you could make it."

Daniel nodded. His smile was still there, but his lips tightened almost imperceptibly.

"Why do you look so constipated?"

Amelia jumped and turned to her brother, who had snuck behind her.

"Is that my cardigan?" she asked.

"Is it?" John looked down. "How could that have possibly happened?"

"I wore it at Christmas. If you didn't steal it, did you buy it to copy me?"

"Oh, my sweet sister. How I've missed you. Can't we talk without all this discussion of clothing ownership?"

She shook her head. "Don't play innocent. I know how you work."

"And yet you still leave your things where I can find them," he said.

John looked stunning, as always. He wore her baby blue cardigan with a pink tank top and fitted jeans. It was such a cute outfit; she wondered if she could take some inspiration from it.

"So, a boyfriend?" he asked.

"Yep." She turned to Daniel, only to find him looking back at her. She waved him over. "Daniel, this is my brother, John."

"Nice to meet you."

"Hey, man. I can't believe you actually came," John said, shaking Daniel's hand. "I thought Amelia was faking it for a while there."

"Ha," Amelia replied dryly. Daniel raised an eyebrow at her. "You think you're so funny."

John beamed. "I could be a comedian."

"I should get our things," Daniel said into her ear. "Be right back."

He returned shortly with the two bags, and her mom trailed behind him. After Amelia grabbed her suitcase from him, her mom asked, "How was your drive?"

"Oh, you know. We just narrowly avoided being sandwiched in between two cars."

Her mom stopped, eyes wide with worry. "Are you okay?"

"Amelia's quick thinking saved us from crashing," Daniel said. "She pulled to the side of the road when someone stopped too fast. The driver behind us didn't react as quickly."

"Oh my God," she muttered, but Amelia was too busy feeling the warmth grow in her cheeks at his compliment. She repeated, "Are you okay?"

Amelia waved her off. "I'm fine. Daniel drove the rest of the way."

"That's good to hear," she said. "I'm glad you had your partner with you to help."

The words felt pointed, as if Amelia needed to learn something from it. She could only fake a smile, trying to keep her nerves at bay.

She was fine being single. She knew that.

"Do you want us to hold the elevator?" her dad called. He'd made it across the parking lot and was waiting for them.

"I'm coming, honey!" Her mom worked her way over to the building.

The bottom of it was on tall wooden beams, with some tenants parking their cars in the empty space. Amelia had learned after many years of coming here that the area often flooded during hurricanes. The condos began on the first floor, and their particular accommodation was on the fourth, at the very top.

The elevator was tiny, and with her three family members and Daniel, plus their luggage, it felt even smaller.

"We can get the next one," she said.

"There's room," her mom assured them. "Come on."

Daniel went in first, and Amelia knew she couldn't easily make an excuse as to why she couldn't join.

It was crowded and hot. She and Daniel were crammed into the front of the space. She had no choice but to lean into him. At first, she thought that she might die from embarrassment, if the hot, sticky hair didn't get to her first. Daniel felt stiff underneath her.

But then his hand settled on her back, and he wound one of his arms around her, pulling her in closer.

Her skin tingled from where she could feel his hand through her shirt.

At least Amelia could claim it was the heat in the elevator that made her cheeks burn, even if it was because of him.

She was glad when the elevator doors finally opened, but as Daniel pulled away to exit, she missed having him nearby. The cool air hitting her skin wasn't anything compared to the feeling of having him close.

Their condo was near the elevator and was always picturesque in the ocean air. The ceilings were tall, with walls painted a light blue. The carpet under her feet was slightly worn from all the families that had stayed here, but Amelia didn't mind.

She was sure the beach decor was gorgeous, but as usual, Amelia's eyes were caught by the balcony. She loved the ocean, and this was her first time seeing it in a year. The water glistened in the sun, pushing waves to the shore. People were either hiding under umbrellas or venturing into the water.

"Which one is our room?" Daniel asked, pulling her out of her thoughts.

"I want the one with the bathroom," she announced.

"Aw, come on," John complained. "I usually get that room."

"There's two of us and only one of you," she said, shrugging.

John muttered something to himself but didn't say anything else. She led Daniel to where they'd be sharing a bed for the next week.

"Yes," she muttered. "He didn't fight me on it. If I had to guess, it would be because you're here."

Save for the master, this was the best room in the condo, with its queen-sized bed and en suite bathroom. The bigger mattress was going to be far more accommodating than the full one that John would be using.

There was a knock at the door, followed by her mom poking her head in. "Sorry to ask so soon after we arrived, but do you two want to go to dinner with us? The three of us are going to walk to the burger place down the road. We discussed it in the car."

Amelia turned to Daniel, who was already looking at her, as if trying to figure out what she wanted.

"We can go," Amelia said. "As long as it's okay with you."

"I'm fine with that," he replied. She scanned his features for any sign that he *wasn't* fine, just like she used to with Andrew. But she couldn't read Daniel the same way.

This thing they were doing was already a ludicrous, unthinkable thing. The last thing she wanted to do was push him too far. She couldn't handle it if he snapped at her and then she had to sleep next to him at night.

"Let me just get John and we'll go." She left the doorway as Amelia tried to calm down.

"Are *you* feeling up to going?" Daniel asked.

"I'm good."

"Are you sure?"

"Yes. Of course I am. None of this is weird at all."

It was *very* weird.

He sighed but then said the last thing she expected. "Am *I* doing something wrong?"

"No!" she quickly reassured him. "You're doing great. Better than I expected, actually. I guess I'm having a hard time shifting into pretending to be in a relationship."

"I'm sure our near accident didn't help. It's been a long day."

"It wasn't *that* bad."

"But it wasn't great. Things don't have to be the worst-case scenario to affect someone. And I feel like I should check on you. It's what any good boyfriend would do."

Would her cheeks ever cool? Even when they didn't have to pretend to be a couple, he was good at finding the right thing to say.

"You're not wrong . . . about any of it. I guess I just hoped this would go smoother."

"We're here in one piece and settled in. I would say things are going well."

"Are you guys coming?" John asked, opening the door. "I run off of delicious food and I'm on empty right now."

"Then we definitely need to go," Amelia said, walking out of the room. "Where are Mom and Dad?"

John groaned. "No idea. They disappeared after saying they were just grabbing something." He turned toward the back of the condo. "Mom! Dad! You coming?"

Their parents came out of their room only moments later, and they began the short walk to dinner. Twice, Daniel's hand brushed hers, and she tried and failed to work up the courage to grab his. Hers would feel so small in his much larger ones . . .

"Daniel, I'm so glad you could join us," her mom said as they got to the sidewalk.

"Me too," he replied. "I've been needing a vacation for a while now."

"Oh, we all do! I worked in customer service for years and I can't stress the importance of a break."

He nodded. His lips pursed and his eyes narrowed, as if he were trying to figure out what to say. Amelia had seen this expression before in meetings that he was told to lead.

"So, how was *your* drive?" Amelia asked, eager to get the conversation flowing again. Daniel gave her a smile, melting her brain into a puddle of incoherent thoughts about how attractive this man was when he did something as simple as *smile*. She fought to keep herself composed and focused on the question she'd just asked.

Even if she'd already forgotten what it was.

"Boring," John said. What was boring again? His job?

Right, their *drive*.

"Oh, stop." Her mom rolled her eyes. "It was uneventful. We were able to drive straight here."

"That's good," Amelia said, nodding. "But you guys didn't have to try to beat us here. We would have been fine had we gotten here first."

"But we were the ones who were told the new entry code for the door," she reminded. "Or at least that's what your dad said. I tried to tell him that we could just text that to you, but I think the rush was actually because your dad was excited to meet Daniel."

"And be relatively near you on the drive, in case something happened," her dad added. "Like a near car wreck."

"Everything *was fine*."

"Thanks to your quick thinking," Daniel added.

Wow, he really wasn't going to let that go, huh?

"Dad had this idea that your car was going to break down like mine did when I tried to drive myself," John explained.

It had not been pretty. That particular year, John wanted to drive himself so he could skip being stuck in the car with Amelia and their parents. After four hours on the road, his car sputtered to death and gave up on going any farther.

"And that was very nerve-racking," Amelia said. "But I do also change the oil in my car."

"It didn't need more oil! The car kept leaking it out!"

"That's . . . not how cars work," Daniel said.

"I mean, I know that *now*." John sighed. "I'm far too pretty to have to worry about changing oil."

Amelia opened her mouth to inform him that it *still* wasn't how the world worked, but her dad opened the door to the restaurant, stopping her before she could even start.

"Okay, my beautiful son, let's go inside and eat. And the rest of us can be grateful you no longer have a car."

Their group piled into the restaurant, and Daniel pulled out a seat for Amelia. Her cheeks exploded in heat. When was the last time anyone had done that for her?

"So, John, how is work going?" she asked after they had a moment with the menus. "I feel like I haven't heard one of your stories in forever."

"Oh, yes. Let's hear about it," her mom encouraged.

John could talk about his job for hours. Amelia used to tire of hearing his wild stories about being a fitness instructor, but she'd been so busy with work lately that she barely had time for anything else—including catching up with her brother—that she welcomed them now.

He began talking about one of his clients, and she was able to listen for the first half of it. Then, a loud family came in, and it was all she could do to keep looking at John. No one else at the table seemed to be bothered.

It didn't get better as time went on. The restaurant only got louder, and she wasn't able to remember a thing John said. She wasn't able to focus, and she knew she couldn't use the earbuds stashed in her purse without Daniel noticing.

Her mind buzzed as they finally left after the meal, and her social skills had rapidly dwindled. She needed to grab Daniel's hand. She needed to pretend to like him so her family would see how happy they were.

And yet, she was stuck.

"Why don't you two go for a walk?" her mom suggested when they returned to the condo. "It's a pretty night. *Very* romantic."

"I'm not sure," Amelia said.

"The beach has always helped you unwind."

She wasn't wrong, but Amelia also didn't know what Daniel might want to do.

"Daniel did half the driving," she said. "He might be tired."

"I'm okay to go," he piped in.

Amelia nodded. "Okay, then. Let's head down there."

They walked through the parking lot and down the brick-laden path to the water. As they got to the dock, Amelia pulled off her shoes.

"It's very nice here." His eyes were on the ocean.

"It's even better when you see the water." She walked ahead, leading him to the waves. The sun was setting on the opposite side of the water, casting the sky with purple and pink hues that painted the background of the hotels. The waves were smaller today, rushing up the sand until it was inevitably pulled back by the next one.

The air was salty, and the wind blew gently through Amelia's hair. This was the kind of sound and sensation that she craved.

"I love it," she said. "I really look forward to this every year. It's not glamorous, but it's still nice."

"Not everything has to be glamorous," Daniel said. "I got enough of that with my ex-wife."

"I'm getting some . . . vibes that things weren't all hunky-dory then."

"Vibes, huh?" he asked with a smile.

"I've had them for a while."

"You're right. But Lucinda wanted us to look a certain way around people, so we spent a lot of time pretending we were fine."

"You're good at it—the pretending, I mean."

"I hope it wasn't too much."

"It wasn't. Just . . . new."

"We'll be learning all kinds of new things about each other on this trip."

Like if he snored. Or had morning breath. Or if he woke up with a—

Nope. Not going there.

"You got quiet at dinner," he said. "Did I do anything to cause that?"

"No," she replied immediately. "It was so loud, and I felt . . . overwhelmed, but I know I need to be better."

"Better at what?"

If it were Andrew, she'd say better at everything. "At being your fake girlfriend."

"I think you're doing fine."

"We should be . . . closer. Like a serious couple would be."

"Oh. You mean *that*."

She glanced at his hands. Never in her life did she imagine she would be close enough to touch them. Now that she needed to, she was still in coworker mode.

"This is weird, isn't it? Like, we've never touched before. Other than the hug, which was . . . nice."

"Yes, it was."

"But *casually*, I don't know how to touch you. Or if you *want* to be touched."

"If I were your boyfriend, what would you do?"

Her mouth went dry.

"I'd hold your hand, maybe."

"Then we start there." He offered her his open palm. For a second, she marveled over the plane of his skin, realizing how surreal all of this felt. For so long, Daniel was only a coworker. There was nothing else.

She slowly lifted her hand and slotted it into his.

It was a perfect fit, something so cruel to discover, considering that none of this was real. She looked back up at him, searching for any hints that he didn't like it. But his eyes were on their hands.

"If it's weird—" she began, but he cut her off.

"This is nice. Just like the hug was."

She giggled, the sound so unusual out of her own mouth. But she couldn't help it. She felt giddy, like a girl being taken to prom, simply from the feeling of his hand in hers.

"I think so too."

CHAPTER EIGHT

DANIEL

Her hand was warm in his, and instead of his heart racing in fear of what Lucinda might say, it was racing for an entirely different reason.

This was something different. Some*one* different. And he liked this, the feeling of her skin on his. He liked every second of it.

"So, were all those stories John told true?" he asked as they resumed their walk over the sand.

"Oh, yeah," Amelia replied. "He's a personal trainer, so I'm sure he sees all sorts of people."

"He's a good conversationalist."

"He definitely is. He could talk forever if you'd let him."

"My sister can be like that. Her name is Terri. She's the extrovert of the family."

"There always has to be one. And then there's the weird one. That would be me."

"And me, if we follow that rule."

"Okay then, tell me something that makes you weird."

"I like sleeping with socks on in the winter."

She froze. "Wait, you *sleep* in socks?"

"My feet get cold." He couldn't sleep if his feet were cold. He hated the feeling, especially when he usually stayed warm.

"So are they like . . . fuzzy socks?"

"No, just my regular ones. I don't like the way fuzzy ones feel in shoes."

"Well, yes, but that's because you don't wear them in shoes. You wear those to sleep, if you can even tolerate the feeling of socks while being asleep." Her free hand gestured as she spoke, and he knew that if he hadn't been holding the other one, it would have been too.

"I thought it was normal to sleep in socks until Terri pointed out that it was a huge debate. And besides, what's the point of having socks that you *only* sleep in?"

"They're like pajamas for your feet."

"That seems like too much to keep track of."

Her jaw dropped. "I can't believe this. You're completely ignoring the beauty of fuzzy little foot pajamas in favor of everyday, probably cotton socks. You *are* weird."

"I tried to warn you."

Her lips twisted, and she shook her head. "I might still have you beat, though."

"Are you sure? Your reaction to my sock habit was pretty intense."

"I'm just a little dramatic," she said. "I still think I have one that's worse."

"I'm more than ready to hear it."

"I never eat sauce with my food. I just scarf it down like a snake with an egg."

"Even chicken?"

"I eat it dry. I didn't even have ketchup with my fries at dinner."

"And you *like* that?"

"I do. If only I could unhinge my jaw too, then I'd really eat like a snake."

Daniel laughed at the sheer absurdity of this conversation. "Okay. You have me beat."

"I told you. And I have even more. But you have to be a level-three boyfriend to unlock those."

"And I'm at one right now?"

"We just got to holding hands. We need to hit third base first."

"Third base?"

"Also known as the level-three boyfriend."

"I thought you meant . . ."

"No, not the typical third base." She shook her head. "No boob touching."

"That's what you consider third base?"

She tilted her head to the side. "Isn't that what it is?"

"I don't think so. Isn't it going all the way?"

"Going all the way, as in penis-in-vagina sex?"

A laugh escaped him. "Yeah, but I didn't realize you would say it like that."

"We're holding hands. I think I can say penis and vagina in front of you now."

He laughed again, realizing he'd missed out on this side of Amelia when he was just her coworker. The conversation paused, but she was looking out at the waves, seeming to consider something.

"So, does she live in Atlanta?"

"Who?"

"Your sister. Sorry, my brain jumped topics. It does that sometimes."

"It's fine. And no, she moved to Nashville many years ago. She loves it there."

"I've been there only once. It was a . . . loud town."

"She lives in the not-so-loud part of it, thankfully. I don't get to visit much."

"Because of work?"

"Yeah. I was surprised that Cheryl even let me come on this vacation, but maybe it's her way of saying thank you for all the late nights I've pulled to get stuff done at work."

"That, and the fact that she likes you, even if she rewards all of your hard work with *more* work in the end. At least, that's what she does to me." She let out a long breath, eyes back on the ocean. "It's not fun."

"It's not, especially when your wife wants you to make more and more money doing it." He wouldn't usually say this much, but there was something about Amelia that made him trust her.

"You would think your wife would want to spend time with you," she muttered, shaking her head.

"She did. She wanted a lot, actually. And a lot of it was impossible to achieve, even if I didn't work sixty hours a week."

"But in this job field, the hours are expected."

"I'm sure I could have balanced it better, but I think at that point, I was happy not to have to."

"I'm sorry," she said softly. "But I know how easy it is to miss the bad signs of a relationship."

Daniel knew it had to be her ex she had mentioned, and he was a little more curious than he should be.

"It's too pretty here to talk about hard stuff," she added. "So, let's not even think about it. Tell me about something you love. Your girlfriend should probably know about that, right?"

***

Talking about light topics made it easy for them to wander for what felt like hours. After the long day, Daniel should have been exhausted, but instead, he only wanted to talk to Amelia more.

By the time they finally made their way back to the condo, the space was dark and quiet.

"I'm going to change," she quietly announced as they snuck in.

He gave her privacy, despite the fact that their room had its own bathroom. He wandered into the kitchen to get himself some water. When he'd finished his glass, Amelia was venturing out of their room.

Her sleep outfit was a simple tank top and shorts. It made sense, considering the condo felt warm, even at night. But he hadn't ever seen this much of her before. Her long, tan legs made his mouth go dry, and he purposefully tried his best *not* to look at the way her ass peeked out of her shorts.

And he was supposed to sleep next to her? He was in trouble.

A lot of it.

"Daniel? Are you coming to bed?" Her wording did nothing for his mind. Her mind must have gone in the same direction that his had because her eyes widened. "I mean to sleep. Not anything else."

"I-I know," he said. "I'll head back now."

Avoidance was the best path in this situation. All he had to do was not think about what he'd just seen, but that proved to be harder than expected.

She followed him into the bedroom, shutting the door softly.

"Sorry if this is awkward."

"It's fine," he lied. "It really is."

"Yeah, definitely. It's not like we're about to share a bed or something. Oh, *wait*. We totally are." Her fingers tapped on her leg nervously.

"Are you still okay with it? I can sleep on the—"

"If you're about to say floor, then it's an immediate no. Who knows how old this carpet is? We're adults. We can share a bed and have it not be weird."

"Right. It's like a sleepover."

"Yes!" she said, eyes lighting up. "We could paint each other's nails and tell stories about boys. Or girls. Or whatever."

He laughed. "I'll take black nail polish. It's the only one that looks good on me."

"You've tried nail polish?"

"My sister had a phase where she thought she wanted to be a nail tech, and I was the only willing participant."

"I would pay good money to see that."

"I'm sure my mom has a photo of it somewhere." His dress shirt was stifling him now that she was smiling in his direction. "I . . . should get changed too. I'll be right back."

Daniel had a full set of pajamas, ones that Lucinda had picked out for him to be classier. He didn't know what to expect from Amelia's family, so he brought his nicer items in case he needed them. Now, he wondered if he had packed too formally. A T-shirt and basketball shorts would have been so much more comfortable.

Amelia was lying in bed, scrolling on her phone. She looked up at him as he crossed through the bathroom doorway. "Oh, those are nice."

"Is it too much?"

"Whatever makes you happy. I'd wear one too, but I lose any sets I get." She shrugged and then went back to her phone.

Nothing seemed to faze her. She didn't look at him and want him to be any different than what he was. It was a nice change.

Daniel slowly sat on the unoccupied side of the bed. She was watching videos on her phone, using some social media app he'd never thought to touch.

"Sorry," she said, "it's an addiction I can't seem to quit. But I've got it finally trained to show me ugly cat videos."

"*Ugly* cat videos?"

"Oh yeah. I mean, look at this." She showed him a hairless cat. "It looks like a turkey. I love it so much."

He laughed. "Do people really have those?"

"Of course. Aren't they cute?"

Cute was maybe the wrong word, but he'd never tell her that. "They're unique."

"I want one," she said, sighing longingly. "Oh! This one has a sweater!"

She showed him another one.

"Does the cat . . . *like* the sweater?"

"Of course. Wouldn't you get cold if you were naked all the time?"

"I run hot."

"And you wear socks to bed?"

"It's unnerving to have my feet cold when I'm otherwise usually comfortable."

"So, you're warm right now? And you're wearing that?" She eyed his formal pajamas. "I mean, you do you. They're very stylish, but I'd hate for you not to sleep because of them."

"I . . . might change," he said.

"You should. Maybe I can borrow those. I always get cold wherever I go."

"And you're sleeping in a tank top and shorts? Not that you *can't*, but—"

She smiled. "It's fine. I used to try to sleep in more, but I would always get uncomfortable if I had too much on, regardless of whether

I was cold or not. Sometimes, I would rip my pants off in the middle of the night. I figured it was for the best that I didn't do that here."

She wasn't wrong, and Daniel refused to picture her sleeping with no pants on. Even if he might have liked it.

Instead, he grabbed the old T-shirt and shorts that he threw into the suitcase at the last second, noting that he might go get more if he needed to. Once he was done changing in the bathroom, he folded up the pajama top and offered it to Amelia.

"You can have these," he said. "Maybe not to wear now, but if you ever wanted them."

"Really?"

"I'd rather someone have them that will use them. And we might be the same size."

"I'll make it work as most girlfriends do," she said, taking them from him. "Even fancy ones. I'll put the top on. And the bright side is, if I rip this off, I have more underneath it. Thank you."

"You're welcome," he replied as he watched her put it on. It looked far better on her than it did him.

"These are so nice. Now I won't be freezing at night. Until I get tired of the extra layer, that is. My brain is weird."

"I think it's fine. I'm glad I could help."

"Yes, thank you." She gave him a smile, looking up at him through her dark lashes. His heart skipped a beat, and he had to distract himself by lying down.

"Okay," she said, putting away her phone, "time to cut myself off from cat videos to get some sleep. Hopefully, it works and I don't go back to scrolling within five minutes."

"Can't stay away?"

"Sometimes, but other times, it's just that my brain won't shut up. A run usually helps."

"You run?"

"Yep." She pulled up the covers. "John trained me for a while. It really helps with keeping me focused. I try to get one in once I catch myself doomscrolling social media."

"Sounds like a good habit. I usually read."

"What do you like to read?"

"I love a good mystery. Sometimes I read science fiction."

"That's amazing. I have a few books, but I can't always focus on reading."

"It's one of my favorite things to do. It really helped when Lucinda . . . you know, left."

"I understand," she replied. "And if you ever need some quiet time to read while we're here, that would be fine too."

Daniel smiled. "I might take you up on that. For now, I think I'm tired enough."

"Same." She turned off the light, plunging them into darkness. He felt relaxed until her leg brushed his under the covers. She jumped away from him. "Sorry," she mumbled.

"It's a small bed," Daniel said. "It's bound to happen."

"Right. I'll still try to keep to my own space. Good night."

"Night," he murmured.

He stayed awake for far longer than he wanted to in the dark, reveling in the heat of Amelia's body and her peony scent. He stayed awake long after her breathing evened out.

Eventually, the warmth dragged him under. And as he fell asleep, he could have sworn he felt her leg touch his again.

But this time, it stayed there.

***

The next morning, he woke up with the sun streaming through their window.

His pajama top was still loosely on her, though one shoulder was exposed, and it was conveniently the one pressed against him.

Thoughts broke out against his will. What would it feel like if he moved his arm and wrapped it around her? What would it be like if she was curled into him, her head on his chest while she slept? It seemed so natural, just like the way holding her hand had felt on the beach.

But they weren't really dating, and he had no right to touch her in a way she didn't ask for. So he gently moved away, taking only a moment to stretch before going to the bathroom. His mind kept circling back to Amelia, and every time it did, his skin tingled from where he'd touched her.

He hopped into the shower, hoping it would take his mind off of her. It drowned out the memory of her shoulder pressing against his, and when he got out, he felt more put together. He reached for his usual hair cream but paused as she once again invaded his mind.

They're very stylish, but I'd hate for you not to sleep because of them.

Technically, slicking his hair back wasn't uncomfortable, but it was annoying to maintain and wash. Without it, however, his hair was messy, and his natural curls would be all over the place.

He considered going without it, but he wondered what Amelia would say. And then what her family would say.

The last thing he wanted to do was deviate from the person Amelia knew him as. After all, she'd asked the normal version of him to do this fake-dating thing.

After putting his hair in its usual style, he got dressed in a polo and khaki shorts, an outfit he considered somewhat formal, and wondered what it would be like to let go, even for just a little bit. He used to never be so worried about his appearance, but it was something Lucinda used to have a problem with.

Amelia was still asleep, so he went out into the main area, hoping to get some water.

"Don't you look nice," Mandy called from across the room.

He turned to face her and felt a slight pang of jealousy. She had been in a nice blouse and expensive-looking tailored jeans yesterday when they arrived, but now, her outfit was casual and ready for vacation life—making him feel overdressed.

"Thanks," he said.

"Are you going somewhere? I'm heading out to get some coffee myself."

"Maybe I should get Amelia something. She loves it in the morning."

Mandy smiled. "You're welcome to join me if you want. There is a shop only a half mile from here."

"Of course," he said. "Lead the way."

Saying yes was the right thing to do, but his heart pounded at the idea of being alone with Amelia's mother. Could he manage not to screw this up? He wasn't so sure.

The minute they were out of the condo, Mandy said, "You know, Amelia didn't even tell me she was dating someone. I was so surprised!"

"It's new," he replied.

"So she said." Mandy pressed the button for the elevator. "I hear you two met at work."

"We did. It was a few years ago."

"So, you've known each other a long time. What made you wait so long to ask her out?"

"I didn't ask, she did. And we were different people when we met."

"How so?"

Normally, he wouldn't answer, but this wasn't a coworker, this was Amelia's *mom*, who undoubtedly only wanted to know how this all happened.

And Daniel wanted to be open with her. He didn't want to be businesslike. Not here.

Not when Amelia herself was so open.

"I was married when we met."

"Oh, really?" Mandy's eyebrows rose.

"T-there was no overlap," he rushed to say. "I would never—"

"I wouldn't dare think that." She waved her hand. "I'm just wondering when this started and why Amelia didn't tell me."

"We only went on our first date a couple of weeks ago."

"So it's *very* new, then."

"Yes. And I hope me being divorced doesn't change how you feel about our relationship."

Mandy frowned. "Why would that change anything? Marriages can end for all kinds of reasons."

"She's your daughter. You're bound to be protective."

"She's also very smart," Mandy added. "And she's grown. She's going to do what she wants to do, even if it's be single for five years. Thank God that's over with, though. I could only meddle so much before she stopped answering my calls."

His heart refused to slow down. This was getting close to a topic he wasn't sure he wanted to talk about. Mandy's meddling was definitely a point of contention that he didn't want to get in the middle of.

"So, how long have you and Randy been together?" he asked, hoping pivoting would be the best solution.

"Oh, we're nearing thirty years," she replied. "We married young."

"Wow."

"Everyone told us we wouldn't last, even our parents, but we put in the work to make it stick, and here we are."

Work. Had he put in enough work with Lucinda? The countless hours at the office had piled up, but he wasn't so sure that he'd done any *emotional* work with her.

Not that she had either.

What would it have been like to be in Mandy's shoes, where both parties were dedicated to making it last? His mind flashed to Amelia. Would she have been?

"I'm glad you were able to," he said, pulling himself out of his thoughts.

"Now, if it's a bad relationship, it's just bad. Like Amelia's last boyfriend. Horrible man."

Daniel almost asked for more details, but he stopped himself. Why did he want to know?

Amelia brought out a different sort of curiosity from him. Never before did he want to know every detail of someone else's life, but he took each one in with an unusual sense of fascination.

Their conversation died down as they walked. He was too far in his thoughts and didn't notice until minutes of silence had passed. He tried to think of something to say to fill the void, but nothing came to mind.

Mandy beat him to it as they walked into the coffee shop.

"This place is amazing," she said. "It always smells so heavenly."

Daniel couldn't help but agree, even though he wasn't a fan of the drink itself. He scanned the menu, wondering what Amelia would even like. The shop had helpful descriptions explaining what drink was what, but it still didn't give him an answer. He'd only seen her with office-brewed coffee.

Mandy stepped into line and ordered. Daniel followed suit, eyes landing on something random. A macchiato, where espresso was on the top and foamed cream was on the bottom.

"Huh," Mandy said, "is that what Amelia likes these days?"

"I always like to surprise her," he replied.

Mandy shrugged and got her finished drink. Daniel grabbed his, wondering if Amelia would even take a sip of it.

"I'm glad she's trying new things. Sometimes, she has an idea of what's best for her, and it's not really what is."

"Sometimes new things can be good." Or he hoped.

They returned to the condo in silence, and Daniel still couldn't think of a thing to say.

"You're a quiet one, aren't you?" Mandy asked.

"People say that, yes."

"I hope it's not us. I know our family can be a lot."

"No, of course not. I'm honored you invited me. It just takes me some time to warm up to people. Some people say I can be a little businesslike at first."

She nodded, and Daniel hoped it was enough.

They entered the condo as Amelia was coming out of their room with messy hair and a sleepy expression on her face.

"What's this?" she asked.

"Coffee. A macchiato, to be exact."

"I don't think I've ever had one," she said, taking it from him.

"It's espresso at the top and cream on the bottom."

She took a sip and her eyes popped open. "Oh, yeah. There's the espresso."

"I think the cream is the reward."

"So it punches me awake and then I get a sweet treat at the end? I think I like this." She smiled and took another sip. "Thank you for getting it for me."

"You were right," Mandy said. "Something new *is* good for her."

His chest loosened. That had been dumb luck, but he would take any point in his favor.

CHAPTER NINE

AMELIA

As she got to the bottom of the cup, Amelia knew she would be ordering a macchiato from now on.

With the caffeine and her medication in her system, she felt wide awake. She thanked Daniel one more time before looking around to see if her mom was still lingering in the living room of the condo. Usually, on vacation, her mom wanted to adventure, even if they'd stayed on Folly Beach many times.

It wasn't like her to stay in, but Amelia had seen it before when her mother's mental health was on a downward trajectory.

"Is everything okay?" Daniel asked. She'd been staring at the door of her parents' room, thinking of all the ways things could go wrong while he was here.

And apparently, he'd noticed.

She bit her lip, wondering what to say. The last time she'd told a significant other of her mom's diagnosis of bipolar disorder, Andrew had thought her mom was . . . crazy.

And Amelia hated that word.

"Yeah, everything is good. Want to go swimming?"

Daniel blinked at the change of subject, but he didn't call her out on it. "Sure."

"All right, let's get changed."

As he walked away, Amelia realized what she'd offered. Swimming meant getting into her next-to-nothing two-piece swimsuit.

As much as she would love to be secure about her body, she found it hard not to look at herself and see things she wished were different. Her weight fluctuations had caused stretch marks on her belly. Her thighs rubbed when she walked. Her boobs were just a bit smaller than she'd like.

Amelia was well aware that she didn't look anything like his ex. And sure, this was for show, but Andrew proclaimed that it wasn't possible for men not to let it show when they were disgusted by a woman they didn't like to look at. It was why she had dieted for so long before leaving him for good.

She walked to their room. Daniel came out of the bathroom wearing a T-shirt and his swim shorts. She tried not to let her emotions show on her face as she pulled out her swimsuit and went to the bathroom.

Her best bet would be not to overthink this, but that wasn't something she was good at. Her brain operated like a well-oiled machine when it had something bad to spiral over, and once the spiral began, it often thought of too many things all at once. She tried her best to ignore the whispers of doubt as she pulled it on, but it didn't work.

She cursed when she realized she didn't have her cover-up. She waited a moment, content to braid her frizzy hair, hoping he would leave the room so she could run out and grab it. It was only delaying the inevitable, but she'd rather have his reaction be in public where, in theory, he'd school his expression.

Eventually, he did leave, and she ran out, throwing her cover-up on before following behind him.

He was applying sunscreen on his toned arms. This was a bad time for her to notice, but she couldn't help it. As he lathered on the cream, she could see every curve of muscle on his arms. Where else was he toned?

And was she going to be able to keep it together long enough to see it?

Amelia tore her eyes away, determined not to make things weirder than they already were.

So what if he was hot? She knew that when she invited him. It was fine. She could easily make it through this trip without acting on it.

She busied herself with grabbing a bag for towels and sunscreen. By then, Daniel had finished his task, too.

"I'll get the rest of my body down by the pool," he said. "Ready?"

Amelia nodded, gesturing for him to lead the way.

It was a hot and sunny day. They found a free pool chair in the corner of the swimming area, where Daniel pulled off his shirt.

Amelia froze. He was even better shirtless. He had lightly defined muscles and a lithe build that she would be dreaming about.

Nope. Don't do it.

She focused on what she needed to do. That was when she knew she couldn't delay the inevitable.

Her cover-up came off and went into the bag. She could feel the sticky air hit her skin, and she purposefully didn't look at Daniel as she rubbed her shoulders.

There was the sound of a whistling catcall, and Amelia's eyes shot up. An old man was looking at her with a lecherous grin on his face.

"Seriously?" she muttered.

Daniel moved closer. "That's unnecessary."

Amelia looked over at him and saw he was glaring in the direction of the man. His body was angled toward her, sending a clear message that she wasn't alone.

Was he being protective? *Over her?*

Why?

A thousand more thoughts fought for attention in her mind.

"Do you need me to get your back?" he asked, looking down at her.

Her mouth went dry at the idea of his hands on her, but she slowly nodded. They gently pressed into her skin, making long, sure strokes on her shoulders and middle back. Everything else around her slipped away, and all she could focus on was how good his hands felt on her body.

Questions came rolling into her mind as her focus snapped.

Could she get him to lotion other parts of her body? Was he this gentle with Lucinda? Would he be like this in *other* places?

But her thoughts vanished in a puff of smoke when his hands stopped on her shoulders. His grip tightened, and he pulled her close. She shivered, despite the heat in the air.

"Can I kiss your neck?" he asked in a low tone.

"Y-yes." The words tumbled out of her. At that moment, he could kiss her *anywhere*. His lips traced her shoulder, and she closed her eyes, wishing she could memorize every second of the moment. He moved upward, his kiss landing right on the sensitive spot of her neck. She let out a surprised gasp.

He went higher, right until his lips were next to her ear. "There," he whispered, "that should send the message."

Her eyes popped open. Message?

Shit. The wolf-whistler. Daniel was sending a message to *him*.

Amelia's heart sank, and she stepped away from him. Of course. This fake relationship was exactly that.

Fake.

Maybe she should have brought her vibrator or something. Then she could take care of these thoughts that refused to leave. But then again, when would she even have time?

"Good idea," she said. "You put on a good show."

His eyes lingered on her face, and she realized he was breathing *hard*. Had he been affected by that too?

"Sorry if it was too far. I just didn't like the idea of you getting hit on like that." His eyes left her, and he rubbed the back of his neck.

"It's fine." More than fine, even. He could easily do it again and she wouldn't complain. "Do you want to get into the pool now? I doubt anyone else will try anything."

Daniel nodded. Amelia wasted no time jumping straight in. She needed the cold rush after what had just happened.

"Refreshing," she said when she spotted Daniel with only his feet in.

"I don't think I can handle cold water like you can."

"Not many people can."

He nodded, and Amelia's brain started to go back to what had just happened by the chairs, but she shook it off.

Instead, she decided to enjoy the water to quiet her brain. She loved swimming, and the feeling of moving in water always calmed her down. She did a few backstrokes, enjoying that the pool wasn't too crowded as she swam around.

When Amelia was finally done, Daniel was still watching her.

"You could get in, you know," she said as she swam over to him. "You adjust to the water over time."

"I will. I was just noticing how relaxed you look. You don't look like that at work."

"Vacation life agrees with me. There's something about being in water that does good things for my brain."

You and your weird brain.

Andrew. That had been Andrew.

"You already looked stressed again," Daniel noted. "Thinking about work?"

Nope. Just my asshole ex that ruined my faith in humanity.

"Things slip in sometimes," she said. "I'm going to do a few more laps to get back into vacation mode."

She swam off before anything else could pop in. The water did its job, and by the time she stopped, she felt the last bits of her sadness vanish.

Daniel had gotten all the way in but didn't look happy about it.

"Now I see why all the adults stay in the hot tub," he muttered.

"What? Can't handle the cold?"

"I usually stay warm. This is odd for me."

"It would be a shame if someone . . . *splashed* you."

"Don't you dare."

It was too late. Spurred on by her own impulsiveness, Amelia threw water on him. He nearly jumped. At first, he attempted to get away from her, but when that didn't work, he tried a different tactic.

His muscled arms wrapped around her, their skin pressing together. He quickly warmed, possibly because of the head-to-toe blush that Amelia could feel crawling up her own body.

"Now you can't splash anymore."

"This is cheating," she protested. "Foul play."

"The only foul play was what you just did. Now, if I let you go, will you be good?"

"What do I get for being good?"

"A pat on the head. Maybe some words of affirmation, like me calling you my good girl. Or my well-behaved . . ."

The rest of his sentence faded away. *My good girl.* She liked that term. Did he talk like that in bed? Was that what he would whisper to her when they—

Nope. Abort thought.

"Not good enough," she said and jumped, plunging them both into the water. Really, it was for the best. The only way for her to wipe their last exchange from her memory was to throw herself under the cold surface.

"I should have seen that coming," Daniel said, pushing his hair out of his face.

"You're used to the water now, though, right?"

"I suppose I am. But I'm not taking that lying down."

"Technically, you were standing until I knocked you over."

He gave her a flat look.

Anxiety poked at her. Maybe she was taking it too far. Maybe she needed to tone it down and be normal for a second.

But then Daniel smiled. "You'll regret this snark when I come up with a way to get you back."

Her heart lifted. "I don't get the vibe that you're a vengeful man."

"When it comes to how cold this water is? I very much am."

She laughed, wondering what he could possibly come up with. She didn't get long to ponder on it because she saw John walking to the beach.

He was dressed to the nines. He had a drink in his hand and a pink, flowy cover-up that didn't do much covering up.

John always stood out in the small town. Most people here welcomed him with open arms.

"John!" Daniel called, his eyes on her brother. Amelia's heart stuttered in her chest.

John came over, letting his designer sunglasses slide down his nose.

"Yes?" he asked.

"Your tag is showing. You might want to tuck it in."

"Oh." John reached behind him for the offending item. "You're a lifesaver. There's a bartender here I want to impress and he would definitely have seen that."

"Happy to help," Daniel replied.

John winked at him before waltzing to the nearby bar.

Amelia let out a sigh of relief.

"You okay?" Daniel asked.

"Me? Oh, yeah, I'm fine. Just, you know, my family is . . . not everyone's cup of tea."

"They're great people," he said. "Real people. There's nothing wrong with that."

"I agree. It's just . . . my ex didn't."

"The infamous ex?"

"Yep. He and John didn't get along."

"That's a shame. Be honest. Was he jealous that John dressed better than him?"

She laughed. "John dresses better than all of us. I bet that cover-up he was wearing was worth more than half my clothes."

"It was designer."

"You know designer?"

"Not me, but Lucinda does."

"Did she leave anything behind? John might take it. He's on a somewhat-tight budget and I bet she'd hate having her things given away."

"She would. I'll check when I get back."

Amelia went to say something else, but a rowdy kid jumped into the pool right in front of them, splashing her in the face.

She sputtered while Daniel laughed.

"That's what you get for splashing me," he said. "Karma."

"Let's go down to the ocean," she suggested. "Maybe there will be less splashing."

"I thought you loved splashing."

"I only love splashing you. Get it right."

She hauled herself out of the pool, excited to feel the sand between her toes. The beach was busy, but there were only so many people this tiny island could hold. She'd heard Myrtle Beach was worse.

Amelia made a beeline for the water, eager to feel the push and pull of waves. When she got in, a larger one crashed over her, nearly knocking her over.

"Is that . . . *fun?*" Daniel called from the shore.

"Why don't you come here and find out?"

His eyes narrowed at the challenge and he cautiously waded into the water.

"The key here is," she said, "to never turn away from the waves. You don't want to get caught looking at the shore when a wave hits you. But when a wave *is* coming, jump up and then turn."

"You just said never to turn."

"If you're staring right at it when it crashes, you get saltwater in your eyes and mouth. It's disgusting."

"So, always watch the waves, jump, and then turn. That's . . . somewhat clear."

"Trust me, it'll be fun."

Another large wave hit them, but this one dumped water on her head. The salt stung her eyes.

"Are you okay?" he asked.

"Oh yeah. This is great."

"So can I laugh now?"

"Absolutely," she said, finally opening her eyes. "That's half the fun. We're both going to look ridiculous."

And she was right. Amelia's braid fell out in the first hour they were in the water. She could taste salt in her mouth, but all she could do was laugh at either herself or Daniel as they tried to jump over the waves.

Daniel didn't fare much better than she did. His hair curled wildly, all product washed out of it, giving her the sight of a man who belonged on a swimsuit magazine cover. Amelia felt like a mess, but he somehow looked perfect while soaked.

"Maybe we should head in to get some food and water," Daniel said after their second hour.

"We have plenty of water here."

"I mean drinkable water," he said, rolling his eyes. She would have wondered if she'd offended him, but the smile on his face said otherwise.

She briefly considered staying to enjoy the ocean even longer. But then she took stock of how she was feeling. Her throat was dry and her stomach was begging for food. She felt a little like an unmaintained car with all its dash lights on.

They went back up to the room and gulped down three glasses of water before she looked for nearby restaurants on her phone. While she browsed options, Daniel showered.

Amelia needed to as well, but all she could think about was food. Before she could pick out a place, John walked into the condo.

"Do you have food options?" Amelia asked.

"Hello to you too."

"Sorry, I'm starving."

"And I'm dejected," John said. "The bartender is *not* single anymore."

"Oh no. That really sucks." She did feel for her brother, but she also saw a listing for pizza that made her mouth water.

"Give me good news. Something to make me happy."

"Do you want Daniel's ex-wife's designer clothes?"

John blinked. "I'm sorry. I don't think I understood that sentence. Daniel's *who* and *what*?"

"Daniel was married. They're divorced and it's finalized now, but he might still have some of her stuff. She was . . . not the greatest person"—her nose scrunched as she thought about her—"and I bet she'd hate to have her clothes given away. She had really nice stuff."

"First off, I would love to ruin a snooty woman's life by taking her clothes, and second, I love how jealous you got when mentioning her."

"What? I didn't get jealous."

"You made a face."

"Well yeah, because she sucks."

"And he's *your* man now."

Her heart raced at the idea. "Okay, maybe. But she also ignored boundaries and came into work to embarrass him, which is not okay."

"That's right. Defend your man. By the way, I approve. He's a major improvement from the trash you dated before."

"You like Daniel? You barely know him."

"Right, but I know you. And you have that giddy, new-love aura around you. Plus, he's been nice to *me*, which Andrew never was."

"You're right about him being nice. But not the other thing. I'm perfectly normal."

John gave her a doubtful look. "You have never been normal. It's what we love about you, but you *stare* at him. It's like he's your whole world. Just seeing you two makes me wish I hadn't sworn off long-term romance for life."

She could have agonized over his words, but her stomach growled. "As much as I love these life talks with you, I think I will die if I don't eat food."

"You're always hangry when you come back from the ocean. What are you wanting?"

"Pizza."

Just as she said it, Daniel came out of their room.

"Pizza sounds good," he said. His hair was wet and a little less styled than usual. Like in the water, she could see his beautiful curls. Food be damned, maybe she could eat *him* instead.

"I thought you were starving," John said.

Amelia blinked. "I am."

"Then let's go," Daniel said. "No need to waste time."

Thank God he hadn't noticed how she had been looking at him, but John had.

"Down bad," he mouthed and then made kissy faces at her when Daniel's back was turned. She flipped him off.

"Come on," Daniel urged, gently putting a hand on her back. "Food calls."

Amelia went willingly, but she couldn't help but notice they'd gotten much more comfortable with each other.

And she was doing a lot less pretending than she expected.

CHAPTER TEN

DANIEL

After a day of enjoying local food and swimming, Daniel was exhausted and fell asleep the moment his head hit the pillow. He didn't have a second to think about the way his arm had touched Amelia's.

But when he woke up, she was all he could think about.

He'd shifted closer to her in the night. Both of them were in the middle of the bed rather than on their respective sides. They weren't quite cuddling, but her cheek was pressed against his bicep and one of her legs was curled around his.

That urge he'd felt the day before, the one calling him to pull her closer, screamed for him to move his arm around hers. He wanted to press his nose into her hair and breathe in both her and this moment.

He shook it off.

These were not feelings he should have for a coworker, not even a coworker who he was pretending to date. He wasn't even a cuddler. With Lucinda, they'd never gravitated toward each other during the night, only away.

Amelia let out a soft noise in her sleep, her leg hiking farther up as she got comfortable. This time, her head lay on his arm. It was then that he realized *another* part of him was *very* interested in this new proximity.

Twisting his eyes shut, Daniel tried to think of everything but her body next to his, but all he could see was how she'd looked in her swimsuit jumping into the pool.

This was not good.

He needed to get away and think. Maybe even jerk off. He wasn't sure which would help more. He just needed to *move* before this quickly got awkward.

Amelia protested as he moved his arm, but thankfully, she fell back asleep.

He nearly ran to the bathroom. He turned on the shower, trying to clear his head, but to no avail. He stepped under the spray of the water, still seeing flashes of Amelia whenever he closed his eyes.

He was attracted to her, there was no doubt about it. He thought of her in a way he shouldn't, yet he couldn't stop it. She was what he wanted.

He didn't have experience with wanting people. He liked Lucinda because she was pretty and seemed smart, but he never felt like *this* about her. He never had to throw himself into the shower simply because she moved closer in her sleep.

Get her off your mind, he begged himself. *Think of anything else.*

But none of it worked. Once he stopped thinking about her body, he remembered the tiny little noise, almost a moan, that she let out as she moved closer.

It didn't matter what he tried to do. She wouldn't leave him.

Daniel wrapped his hand around his length, but he made one rule.

Don't think about her. Get this over with but leave her out of it.

The rule seemed simple in theory but difficult in practice. As his hand moved, he tried to think of anyone else he'd been attracted to.

No one came up.

He then decided to think of nothing, only the sensation in his body as he moved himself closer to release. His hand moved up and down his cock, his mind focused only on how it felt. He could feel himself getting closer.

His mind replayed how her skin had felt as he rubbed her back, except this time, he was only doing it for *himself.* He could see him taking her back to their room, her under him, as he kissed his way down her chest, her stomach, and then to her—

He came.

And then immediately hated himself for it.

That was not what he was supposed to do. He'd broken his one rule right at the last second.

Leaning his head against the bathroom wall, he sighed. No more of this. This was the *one* time he would allow himself to ever do that. The last thing he wanted was to be a creep.

Daniel cleaned himself off and got dressed for the day. He barely put any cream into his hair, his mind too distracted by what he'd just done.

Maybe he needed fresh air.

That should solve it.

He went to the balcony, where the wind was blowing and the call of the waves was loud, and sat.

That was when his phone rang. He pulled it out and his mood plummeted further.

It was his father.

"Hello?" Daniel answered, his voice sounding more annoyed than he wanted it to.

"My boy! I have some good news."

"What?" Daniel rolled his eyes. He was unable to keep the frustration from seeping into his voice. Thank God he was alone for this. The last thing he needed was for anyone to overhear his tone and ask questions. Just how was he supposed to admit to Amelia's family that his wife had left him for his *father*?

"Lucinda said yes to marrying me."

His ears rang as his father spoke more.

Lucinda and his father were getting married? Only four months after Daniel and Lucinda's divorce was finalized? This couldn't be real. His father couldn't be *that* cruel.

Then again, his father *did* sleep with her in the first place. Staying as boyfriend and girlfriend wouldn't last for long. His father wanted a trophy wife, someone beautiful to parade around in his church.

Lucinda wanted money, which her soon-to-be husband had plenty of.

"So, what do you say, son?" he asked.

Daniel blinked back into the present moment. "What?"

"Are you coming to the wedding?"

"*What?* You want me to come to my ex-wife's wedding? To you?"

"I thought it would be helpful for moving on from her."

Daniel couldn't believe his ears. "No, I don't want to go."

His father sighed, as if he expected this. "Daniel . . ."

"No."

"You need to move on from her, son."

"I have moved on," Daniel said. "I am literally at the beach with my girlfriend right now."

"Oh, well, what's the problem?"

"You still slept with my wife. While we were married."

His father sighed. "We talked about this."

"No, *you* talked about it," Daniel said. "I don't want to be a part of this."

"You have to be. What will people say if my own son is not at my wedding? It will be televised, and millions of people will watch."

Daniel shook his head. "No, I don't care what people think, and besides, your daughter won't even be there. You're not inviting Terri."

"She strayed from God."

"And adultery isn't straying from God?"

"I atoned for that."

Daniel took a deep breath, resisting the urge to throw his phone off the balcony.

"I'm not going," he repeated. "And I'm not changing my mind about it."

"You're still hung up on Lucinda, then?"

"I *just* said I'm dating someone else."

"Does she know about your ex-wife? It's okay to still be in love with your ex, especially when she's a woman like Luc—"

"I'm not in love with Lucinda. I'm not sure I ever was, but that doesn't mean I want to come to the wedding. Now, please leave me alone. I'm currently on vacation with my *girlfriend*, who I actually like, trying to have a good time."

Daniel hung up angrily, gripping it tightly as he tried to get his emotions under control. Minutes passed, and just as he was finally beginning to breathe normally, he received a text.

Lucinda: Who's your new girlfriend?

His jaw tightened again. Why did she even care? Didn't she have the happy ending she wanted?

Of course not. She wouldn't be satisfied until she knew he missed her.

The balcony door opened, and for a second, Daniel thought Amelia had woken up and come and found him. Instead, it was John.

"Hey," John greeted.

"Hey," Daniel repeated back, letting out a breath and trying to sound normal.

John looked at him quizzically. "Are you okay?"

"Not exactly." There was no point in lying. "But it's nothing involving your sister, I promise. You don't have to kill me or anything."

"If you pissed off Amelia, I'd let her do the killing anyway. Want to talk about it?"

"I'd rather not."

"Then . . . would coffee cheer you up?" John asked. "If you're dating Amelia, then you're probably into coffee, right? I mean, I don't exactly know about how relationships work, but you have to have *something* in common."

Daniel laughed despite his sour mood. "No, I'm more of a tea drinker, but maybe going down to the coffee shop would help."

"I'll go with you," John said. "I need my caffeine anyway."

Daniel nodded. He needed to get his mind away from everything that had happened in the last hour.

"So," John started as they walked down the stairs, "should we do some kind of small talk?"

"We can. I'm not very good at it, though."

"Me either. Especially with guys my sister dates. I mean, there was only the one, but still. I knew he didn't like me."

"Why didn't he?"

"I'm going to go with the fact that I have more skirts than Amelia does. Some people don't like that."

"Oh."

"She tried to hide it, but I saw it. It's kind of hard not to. So, good on you for not being like him."

"You're a person first and foremost. None of the rest matters to me."

"See? You get it. My family does too. I think Amelia had bad luck with him."

"We all have to have one bad ex."

"Not me. I don't usually date," John said, rolling his eyes. He opened the door to the coffee shop, and Daniel stepped in. He glanced at the menu, deciding to take another risk and pick something new for Amelia.

"Ooh," John said. "The barista is cute. How do I look?" He turned to Daniel expectantly.

John looked better than most people in the coffee shop, with one exception. "Are you wearing mascara?"

"Yes. Is it too much?"

"No, it's just smudged."

"You're a lifesaver," John said before putting on a picture-perfect smile.

Daniel tried not to listen as John flirted with the man, but it was almost impossible. After successfully getting the barista's number, John put in his order.

"Oh," John said. "And his order is on me."

"What?" Daniel asked. "You don't have to—"

"You're the first potential brother-in-law I *like*. Plus, I owe my sister a coffee."

"Since when?"

"Since I was a pain in her ass in high school. I try to make up for it sometimes. Now, tell the gorgeous man what you both want."

Daniel didn't argue but thanked John after he paid for the order.

As they headed back to the condo, John was already shooting a message to the barista, and Daniel took a moment to process all that had happened this morning.

He had to tell Terri what had gone down with their father. She'd want to know.

When they got to the elevator, Daniel gave John Amelia's drink. "Mind giving this to your sister? I have a family call I need to make."

"Oh, sure. You do what you have to."

Once John was in the elevator, Daniel found a small table to sit at and sent his sister a message.

Daniel: Are you free? I need to call you.

A few minutes later, his phone rang.

"What's up?" Terri asked.

Telling her the news needed to be like ripping off a Band-Aid. "Dad and Lucinda are engaged."

"What the *fuck*?" Terri said slowly. "Seriously?"

"Yes."

"How did you find out?"

"He just called me."

Terri made a sound of disgust. "I hate him. I hate him so much. Honestly, Daniel, this is awful of them, but not surprising. Dad's been wanting a trophy wife for a while."

"Yeah, but he didn't have to take *my* wife."

"No, he didn't, but you have to admit, Lucinda is the kind of person who wants to be someone's trophy."

Daniel sighed. He'd felt the sharp sting of betrayal when he'd first found out, and while this still hurt, he was glad Lucinda was getting exactly what she wanted.

If only she would leave him alone to do it.

"I just thought you should know," he said.

"Do you want any advice?"

"Not really. I mean, I have enough sense to know it's wrong, but that doesn't make it any better."

"It doesn't," Terri said. "I'm sorry."

"It's okay." At that moment, a child ran past. His voice was loud as he yelled for his sibling to give something back.

"What was that?"

"A kid," Daniel said, sighing.

"Wait, are you at the beach right now?"

"I am."

"So, you did go!" Terri laughed. "Finally! Some good news! How is it going?"

"It's . . . something, that's for sure."

"Tell me about Amelia."

"She's . . . hard to describe."

"In a bad way?"

"No, not at all," he said. "She's . . . incredible."

"Incredible, huh? I need some details."

"She and her family have been welcoming. They're all so close-knit, but very welcoming."

"That's good. At least it's not drama central. Are you having fun?"

"Yes. Amelia is fun in a way I'm not used to." She was *many* things he wasn't used to.

"Can you see herself dating her?"

"In a fake way? Yes."

"Come on, what about a real way?"

"I just got divorced."

"Sure, but you can look. Maybe this fake relationship can turn into a real one."

"She said she doesn't do relationships."

"Fine. Then a rebound?"

"Not with a coworker."

"Ugh. I just want you to move on. Call me when you sleep with someone," Terri said. "Wait, maybe don't. Maybe wait, until like, *after*."

"That is not something a normal sister would say."

"When was I ever normal? I just want you to find your fairy tale happy ending, that's all."

"For now, my happy ending is paused until I see how Dad announcing his new fiancée will go."

"Fair enough. Then just have fun. Go mini golfing. Just keep your head on and try to enjoy yourself. That's what I did when I got lost in South Dakota."

"I thought it was Montana."

"Oh, it was multiple states," she said. "But this is good. It sounds like this might be a real vacation for you."

"Yeah, maybe it is," he said, nodding. "And maybe I do need to be more like you."

"Well, you won't really be like me until you fall in love on one of those adventures. But I'll give you a few years to catch up on that one," she joked. "Seriously, though—I'm glad you're okay."

Daniel smiled. "Thanks, Terri."

"And call me if anything interesting happens. I swear, I always wanted you to do something like this. It's better than reality TV."

CHAPTER ELEVEN

AMELIA

"He said he wanted to be alone?" Amelia asked, frowning over her coffee. John had been the one to deliver her a caramel latte this time but said Daniel had chosen it. She wanted to thank him since John had made it clear that Daniel had gone with the specific intention of getting something for her.

"Yeah, I think something is going on with his family. He seemed a little mad."

Shit. Anger wasn't a good emotion.

Maybe it was her. Maybe she got too close to him in the middle of the night. She'd woken up in the center of the bed, after all.

"Amelia," John said, taking in her expression, "I'm sure he's fine."

"Yeah, me too," she lied. Her feet itched to go downstairs and find him. But he said he needed time, and she would give him that. "I think I'm going to go on a walk on the beach to clear my head."

While walking along the shore, she didn't find the clarity she was in search of. Usually, she liked being alone, but this time, it felt empty, like something was missing.

She turned. Maybe she needed to head back to the condo and scroll on social media. Or she could try reading again. Anything to get her mind off this worry that she had somehow messed this up with Daniel.

As she got back, she saw him sitting at a table near the pool. Her eyes caught on him, and he looked up right as she walked toward him.

But she didn't see his facial expression. She saw his *hair*. It was free from its prison of styling, and it flew wild in the windy air. She'd seen this yesterday when they were in the water, but it was another story when dry and windswept.

"Hey," he said. "I hoped you liked your coffee. I took another guess."

"Your hair," she managed to say.

"Oh, this. Yeah, I had an off morning, so I didn't style it. If it looks bad, I'll go inside and—"

"No," she said. "It looks *fantastic*. You should wear it like that more often."

"Really?" He reached up to touch it. "It can get a little frizzy, but it's so much easier to have it like this."

His cheeks were red, and Amelia stopped herself from blurting out anything else about how damn perfect he looked.

She took a deep breath, trying to get her heart to calm down. "Thank you. For the coffee, I mean. I loved what you got me. You guessed my usual order."

"Really?"

"It was spot-on. Nice work. But I think it was *too* caffeinated. Now I'm all jittery." And it definitely *didn't* have anything to do with how one curl had landed on his forehead. *Nope.* Not at all. "And sometimes when I'm jittery, it feels like the world is about to end or something."

It didn't make sense, and she didn't expect Daniel to take it seriously.

But his hand rested on her arm. "It's okay. Everything is fine." His eyes shot up toward the balconies for a split-second. Then his eyes fell back to hers. "Come here."

Pulling her close, he pressed his lips to her forehead. Her face exploded in heat, yet her heart calmed down. How was he doing this?

It seemed impossible, but she didn't want to leave the warm cocoon of his arms. Her body leaned into his as the last of her tension escaped her muscles.

"That's it," he said. "Everything is okay."

"Thank you."

"Just in time for your mom to come out on the balcony too."

Amelia looked up, realizing that it had all been for show again. "Oh, good call."

Her mom waved and Amelia did the same, forcing a smile on her face. She should've been happy about this. He was doing exactly what he was supposed to.

And yet, she wished it had been only for them.

"John mentioned that he doesn't date. Is your mom as hard on him as she is you?"

"Not really," she said. "Which is weird now that you mention it. Why do I have to fake date someone in order to get her off my back?"

"It's a good question."

"I'll ask her once we stage our breakup in a few weeks." Because that was coming, even if she was beginning to dread it.

"After our breakup. Of course."

She could have sworn she caught a hint of disappointment in his voice, but maybe she was projecting her own feelings.

"Are you hungry?" he asked. "We could go get breakfast."

"Food does sound nice." Especially since she'd just taken her medication. "Let's walk down the block. I know a cute place."

They walked to the Front Porch Café, which was a dog-themed breakfast joint. It featured all kinds of delicious breakfast foods with paintings of dogs everywhere.

It was a good meal. She told Daniel some of John's best moments from their childhood, and he shared some about his sister too.

When they got back, the condo was quiet, but her mom's purse was where it had been that morning. Amelia frowned. Usually, they went out and about. Now that she thought about it, her mom hadn't been dressed when she saw her on the balcony.

Amelia peeked into the master bedroom and saw her mom asleep, even though it was almost noon.

It worried her whenever her mom would get like this. When she was a kid, she didn't understand why her mom would be doing a million things at a time one week and nothing the next.

Then she figured out it was bipolar disorder, what used to be called manic depression.

Amelia hated thinking about what her mom went through mentally, and for the longest time, she thought she didn't need to worry about it. She'd never had manic episodes like her mom did. She never went weeks without wanting to sleep. Sure, she had moments where she did all the cleaning and organizing in the world, but she would stop halfway through. That made her normal, right?

Only it didn't. Amelia hadn't inherited the bipolar disorder from her mom, but she had something different. In Amelia's case, it was ADHD.

When she'd heard about it, she thought it was a childhood disorder that didn't really affect adults.

But she couldn't help but notice how messy and chaotic her life had become. She couldn't focus on anything she wanted to. She had sensory issues. And her ADHD was what ruined her last relationship.

This was what she didn't want Daniel to see. This is what would make him change his opinion of her forever.

"Did your mom go back to sleep?" he asked as he walked into the condo. "Is everything okay?"

"Um, yeah," Amelia lied. In reality, her mom would more than likely be down for a bit and then come out of it since she was on medication. But it was always noticeable. She glanced outside to see her dad on the balcony. "I think I'm gonna go catch up with my dad for a minute. Is that okay?"

"Sure," Daniel said. "I'll be in our room."

She nodded and stepped outside. She sat next to her dad who was reading a book and looking calm. He was always like this—he never seemed worried, and Amelia felt like her whole life was a ball of stress.

"Hey, is Mom okay?" Amelia asked.

"I think so. She reduced her medication a few weeks back, so this is to be expected."

"Why did she reduce her meds?"

"They started making her dizzy all the time," he replied. "And she's been feeling better, just a little up and down."

"Oh." She bit her nail. If she'd known, she wouldn't have bothered to ask Daniel to come with them.

"Why do you look worried?"

"Daniel doesn't know about all of . . . this."

"I thought you two were dating." He raised an eyebrow.

Amelia doubted she would have told him even if they were really dating.

"We are," she said, the lie tasting like acid in her mouth. "But he still doesn't know."

"Amelia, mental health is important. He should know."

"I told you guys this was new."

"I know it's new, but I figured he would at least be aware of what was going on."

"I can't exactly tell him that my mom has bipolar disorder on the first date."

"You're not on the first date anymore, are you?"

She didn't have an answer for him because he was right. Maybe if she hadn't seen how Andrew reacted, she would have given it a shot. Maybe if she had any faith left in people, she would have been honest.

"Amelia, I love your mother despite her mental health," he said. "I loved her before she was on medication for it, and I love her now. Having any kind of diagnosis doesn't doom a couple."

"It did with Andrew."

Her dad sighed. "Andrew had his own problems that ruined that relationship. I don't know him all that well, but I can already tell Daniel is different than Andrew."

"I don't know that for sure yet."

Her dad looked at her, eyes slightly narrowed. "You'll have to find out eventually if this is going to go anywhere."

Amelia gritted her teeth, trying to keep from admitting the fact that she knew this wasn't going to go anywhere, that this was all a sham and set up to get her mom off of her back.

He could sense her frustration, just like he always did. "I'm not going to push you on it. I just hope that one day you will feel comfortable enough to tell him and that he doesn't let you down. Not everyone is Andrew."

Amelia shrugged. "Sometimes it feels like it. Most doctors don't even know that women show different symptoms than men, who usually get diagnosed far earlier than women. I still hear people at work call themselves bipolar when their mood slightly changes. I don't trust people not to think I'm . . . crazy . . . when they find out. Or think I'm faking it."

He nodded. "And you're right. The world isn't ready, and they have some extremely uneducated opinions on what bipolar disorder and ADHD are, but it doesn't mean Daniel is one of those people."

"I guess." Amelia gave a shrug as she looked out over the ocean.

"I'm not saying you need to tell him before you're ready," he continued. "But don't just assume he's going to act like Andrew."

She nodded. If this had been real, her dad's advice would have been good. But this wasn't. Daniel was her coworker, and he had no reason to be kind about her ADHD. He had no reason to even care.

"Your mom's going to be okay," he said after a moment. "She just needs a little time."

She knew that he could take care of her mom. He had always been the calm one of the family. He didn't have knee-jerk reactions, nor did he ignore issues that he needed to address. He was almost the opposite of her mom. They balanced each other out.

It was what Amelia had hoped she would have with Andrew.

"Thanks for letting me know," she said. "I better get back to Daniel."

"Any time, kiddo."

Amelia went back inside, still feeling nervous about Daniel seeing all of this, but when she closed the door, she took a deep breath, trying to channel her dad's easygoing attitude.

Daniel was reading. He looked up, worry still etched on his face.

"My mom is fine," Amelia said. "Just tired. We all get like this on vacation. It's like the sun saps all of our energy."

He nodded and put down his book. "I'm glad to hear that. Maybe we should let her rest, though. I'd hate to accidentally wake her up."

"We could go swimming again," she offered, glad Daniel seemed okay with letting her mom have time to rest.

"Maybe the kids went in for lunch," he said. "So we won't get splashed this time."

CHAPTER TWELVE

DANIEL

The kids were not gone. In fact, it was worse than the day before. The pool was completely taken over by Marco Polo.

"There are a few spots left in the hot tub," Amelia said. "We could go there."

Even though the hot tub was more crowded than he wanted, Daniel would rather face that any day.

The warm water encased him as he got in. Amelia followed suit, her thigh brushing his as she sat.

"S-sorry," she said, her cheeks pink. "I can get out if I'm too close."

"It's fine," he replied. "I'm not bothered."

And he wasn't. He craved having her closer, but he was afraid of what might happen if she saw how much it affected him.

Mercifully, the water covered both of them. As long as he didn't think about her for too long, he would manage not to embarrass himself.

But she was nearly knocked into him as someone else forced their way into the hot tub. She pressed against him tighter, but he could see she didn't like having a stranger in her personal space. Daniel felt her hips turn away, so she was sitting at an angle, but it still wasn't enough room.

He had an idea. A very bad one.

"Amelia," he said. He had to lean in to say the words right into her ear because of the noise of the hot tub. It made saying her name feel more intimate than it was. "You could . . . sit on my lap."

"What?" she asked.

"It would give you more space."

She looked at the stranger, who was loudly talking to the person they were with. "Are you sure?"

No. "Yes."

Amelia bit her lip before slowly moving over, lifting her hips and planting them on his legs. He wrapped an arm around her to keep her from floating away.

But then, as she settled, he realized just how bad of an idea it was.

"Well," she said, leaning back so he could hear her. "I definitely have more room. Your lap is comfortable."

He pressed his lips together. He could feel the curve of her ass against his cock, which knew exactly what was going on. Her words did nothing but send blood downward.

"Are you okay?" she asked. "I'm not too heavy for you, am I?"

"No, not at all," he said. "It's nothing."

Maybe she wouldn't move her hips back and feel it. Only then could he get out of this with his dignity intact.

But then someone else wanted to get out of the hot tub. Amelia jerked back to give them room, and her butt rocked against his hardness.

He felt her freeze.

"Sorry," he said. "I didn't expect this to happen here."

She was silent for a long time, and he wondered if she was planning her escape route. He wouldn't blame her.

"I-It's fine," she said, her voice higher than usual. "This is just a thing that happens with friction, right?"

It's you, he wanted to say. *One look at you and I get like this.*

But he gritted his teeth and nodded. For a second, they simply sat. Daniel knew he was too scared to move, despite his mind begging him to rock up and get more delicious friction.

"I can't look at strangers when we're like this," she said. "I'm going to turn around."

Before he could say no, she got up and whirled around where she was facing him. Her legs pinned him in. Instead of his hardness being against her backside, however, it was now pressed against her inner thighs.

"I think this is worse," he said, unable to look at her.

"I'd rather look at you than the other couple rubbing up against each other," she muttered.

The water rippled as someone else got into the hot tub, and it made her move just enough to make his head spin.

"I'm sorry," she said. "I could get out."

"No."

"Well, this isn't comfortable for either of us."

"It's not that its uncomfortable, Amelia," he said lowly. "It's that . . . never mind." The last bit of his control kept him from speaking.

"No, what?"

That control flew out the window. "The only thing that's uncomfortable is that we're surrounded by strangers."

"And if we were alone?"

"We wouldn't be here."

"But if we *were*?"

Did she want him to admit it? They weren't supposed to be like this.

But he also wouldn't lie to her.

"There wouldn't be swimsuits." He muttered the words, hoping that she somehow wouldn't hear them. But her breath hitched and her eyes went wide.

"Really?"

"With a woman like *you*? Can you blame me?"

She *should* blame him. She should tell him no and send him tumbling down to Earth. Being in the clouds was dangerous.

Amelia stared at him, face unreadable.

She's your coworker, his last bit of sense said. *Stop this.*

"We should go to the beach," he said. "I bet it isn't as busy there."

"M-maybe that's a good idea. I'll go first so you can . . . Yeah."

She got out, and Daniel stared at a palm tree rather than her beautiful body. It took him twenty minutes of thinking of anyone but her for his cock to get the message.

Amelia was probably uncomfortable with what had happened. He deserved a lecture from her, or worse, anger. He wouldn't fight it because he should have controlled his body's reaction to her proximity.

After he'd calmed down, he slowly made the walk of shame. She was sitting on the beach, teeth biting at her lip.

"Hi," he said.

"Oh, hey," she replied. "Everything back to normal now?"

"Yes. I'm sorry about that."

"No, don't be. I should have thought about it more before sitting on your lap. But I've always had poor impulse control."

"You're not mad?"

"Mad? Why would I be mad? If anything, I'm flattered. At least some parts of you think I'm attractive."

"All parts of me think you're attractive," he corrected.

But her expression made him want to say it again. Her cheeks turned an exquisite shade of pink, and one corner of her lip turned upward.

"That's sweet." She tucked a piece of hair behind her ear. "You're really good at this fake-boyfriend thing."

He pressed his lips together at the reminder. "It's what I'm here for."

"I'll be sure to return the favor once we're back at the office," she said. "But for now, maybe we could hunt for seashells?"

There was a part of him that wanted to beg her to go back in that hot tub and never leave. He knew he'd never be able to get the feeling of her sitting on his lap out of his mind. But she'd been gracious enough about it already, and she was making it clear that they weren't going to go any further.

"Sure," he said, smiling. "I'll let you know if I see any good ones."

They separated, eyes on the sand. He tried to look for shells, but his mind was distracted.

"Got one!" Amelia called minutes later. She picked it up and showed it to him. "Amazing. All these waves and it still made it here safely. It was resilient."

"Some things truly are," he said.

Her lips pressed together, and he couldn't help but wonder what she was thinking as she stared at the shell in her hands. She took a shaky breath and looked up at him.

"Ready to go swimming?" she asked.

"Don't you want to keep the shell?"

"Nah." She bent and set it on the ground. "I'll leave it for someone else. I just like to look for the fun of it."

It took him a moment to follow her to the water. He tried to figure out what had been going through her head as she'd gazed at the shell, but nothing came to him. Eventually, he followed, wondering what could possibly haunt her as it had.

***

Their swimming was cut short by a pop-up storm. They'd gotten out of the water once the waves became too choppy to be enjoyable, and soon after, rain poured from the sky.

The walk to the condo was cold, and Daniel was grateful to peel off his wet layers. Amelia took solace in the bathroom, and he made quick work of changing before she came back out. He'd had enough embarrassing moments in one day. They didn't need any more.

She came out just as the front door opened. "I brought food!" Randy called as he took off a rain jacket.

That got everyone into the kitchen, even Mandy, who had still been in her room when Daniel and Amelia got back. Daniel didn't miss the way Amelia's eyes lingered on her mother, and he wondered, not for the first time, if everything was as okay as she'd said it was.

"What did you get?" John asked.

"Mostly pizza," Randy replied. "But I got a burger for you, dear." He gave Mandy a kiss on the cheek, which earned him a lukewarm smile.

Those were the things he missed doing for someone. The little things. Lucinda had grown bored of those quickly.

"How about we have dinner and ride out this storm with a movie night?" Randy offered. The condo didn't have room for a table, so they all sat on the sectional couch and ate. They put on an easy-to-watch Disney movie in the background.

"I remember when this came out," Randy said as it played. "This was the only movie Amelia and John could watch together. Everything else, you two fought over."

"I can't help it that he has no idea what's good," Amelia said, shrugging.

"Says the woman who had a *Barney* phase."

"When I was a *toddler*," she muttered, her cheeks turning pink.

"It lasted until you were eight," Mandy added. It was the first Daniel had heard her speak in a while.

"Mom! Whose side are you on?"

Mandy laughed. "The truth's. You really loved that purple dinosaur."

Amelia shook her head. "I can't believe this. In front of Daniel and everything." She turned to him. "Please say you had an embarrassing show too. We need to make it even."

"I grew up with a *lot* of *Veggie Tales*," he said. "It backfired. I didn't eat vegetables for years because I thought it would hurt them."

"Aw, that's adorable." Amelia bumped her shoulder with his.

"I would have loved it if you guys had a Disney phase," Mandy mused. "The songs are so cute. It's a shame you only liked the one movie from them."

"We can't help it that we have taste," John said. "Well, at least I do. Amelia, I'm not so sure about you."

"Very funny. I don't even watch a lot of TV. I don't have time for it with work."

"They do keep us busy," Daniel added.

"Mostly complaining about the same five things," she muttered.

"That's right, you met at work," Mandy said. "Have they been okay with the transition?"

Amelia glanced over at him, and he could see the silent question in her gaze.

"It's new," he said. "But neither of us manages the other, so we haven't run into any issues."

"And there isn't a rule against it," Amelia added. "Unless I missed it in the employee handbook."

"Don't worry too much about work," Randy said. "This is a vacation. A relaxing one, hopefully."

Amelia smiled. "It's been nice for us. What about you, Mom?"

"I've just been tired, but I'm still enjoying it." She returned a small smile to Amelia.

"Hang on," John said, interrupting them. "We can't talk over this song. It's the only Disney one that I like."

They all went back to watching the movie, but Daniel could see that something was bothering Amelia. It could have been anything from their encounter in the hot tub to the relationship disclosure form waiting for them when they returned to Atlanta.

But judging by the way Amelia looked at her mother, he had one strong guess as to what it was.

CHAPTER THIRTEEN

AMELIA

Amelia's brain had an unhelpful way of working through problems.

She'd been trying to find a way to tell Daniel about her mother's bipolar disorder without making him think the dreaded C-word. She got close to a delicate way of phrasing it as she lay awake that night.

By the time she'd drifted off, she knew exactly what she was going to say.

So then she dreamed about it. And dreams were not helpful. In her slumber, Daniel hadn't taken it well at all. In fact, he'd left *early* to avoid dealing with her unsteady family.

When she woke up, she was left with a distinct feeling of hurt that wasn't even real and shock that Daniel was very much asleep next to her.

Rolling out of bed, she ran her hands through her hair, trying to separate dreamland from reality. She was in desperate need of coffee.

She walked into the kitchen and started the coffee pot. When it was done brewing, she headed out to the balcony with a steaming mug in hand. The thick air promised a hot day ahead, but it was tolerable with a fresh morning breeze.

Amelia only sat by herself for a moment before the door opened and her mom joined her. She was more put together today, but the dark bags under her eyes told Amelia that she wasn't sleeping well.

"Hi, sweetheart," she said, sitting. "Your dad told me you might be worried about me."

"I'm okay," she replied.

"And that Daniel doesn't know?"

Amelia looked down at her coffee. "Don't worry about it."

"Why doesn't he?"

"It's complicated."

"Because of Andrew?"

Amelia pressed her lips together and gazed out into the distance. She could see waves crashing on the shore. She could hear people talking on their walks.

"Amelia," her mother started, "all I want is for you to be happy. You know that, right?"

"I do."

"And if anyone ever makes you feel unsafe, then you don't have to be with them."

She clenched her jaw. She wasn't with Daniel—not really. But she was starting to realize that lying about a relationship was worse than being pressured into one.

"I know," she replied. "I'm fine, Mom. I promise."

"You deserve the world. I mean it."

Amelia nodded, but she knew the only good part of the world was her family. The rest was a dark and cold place where she would get judged for things that were outside of her control.

She'd learned her lesson. *Never trust other people.* It had served her well.

But she didn't expect anyone else to understand.

"Thanks," she said. "I'll keep it in mind."

Her mother nodded. "Now, I promised your dad that I would at least try to get out of the condo today. Do you want to join us this evening? There's a live band playing at one of the taco shops."

"I'll try," she replied.

"That's all I ask."

After her mother went back inside, Amelia let out a long breath. She felt off, and the day had barely begun. She probably needed to take it easy, but it was hard to when she knew Daniel wouldn't understand *why*.

"Hey," a deep voice brought her out of her thoughts. She turned, seeing the very man she'd been thinking of peering from the doorway.

"Morning," she greeted.

"Good morning," he replied. "I was thinking about running to Target on the mainland. I need stronger sunscreen. Do you want to come? I'll get us breakfast."

The thing was, she *did* want to go. There was nothing better than a Target run when she was in the mood for it.

"Sure," she said. "Let me just get dressed."

She got up, ignoring the red flags in her mind. Going shopping was not a huge deal. If she could handle getting to work every day, then she could go get some sunscreen.

What was the worst that could happen?

***

As it turned out, the worst thing that could have happened was being followed by a screaming child.

It wasn't that she didn't like kids, but she didn't like loud noises. Her eyes nearly watered at the high-pitched screaming. That, plus the fact that it was packed to the brim with people, had Amelia regretting everything.

Breakfast had been fine. Even driving had been fine. But now she was realizing that it had all lulled her into a false sense of security.

Daniel had grabbed her hand. When he did, she couldn't form a single sentence—not even a thank you. But she could easily agonize over how stupid she must have looked, needing her fake boyfriend to hold her hand in a busy Target so she wouldn't get lost.

By the time they got out and were walking to the car, her ears were ringing from all the noise.

"How was it so busy on a weekday morning?" Daniel grumbled. "Shouldn't more people be at work?"

"Vacation town," she muttered. Her head was *pounding*.

"I should have just stayed on the island and bought a more expensive one," he said. "Sorry for dragging you out in this."

She climbed into the passenger seat. "It's fine."

It wasn't his fault. She was the one who'd gone with him, even though her brain wasn't working with her. She should have bowed out. She leaned her head back on the headrest and tried to calm down, but her brain felt like static.

"Are you okay?"

"I'm fine." It was a lie, but how else could she explain it in a way that didn't make her seem . . . crazy.

Amelia could feel his eyes linger on her for a moment, and she wanted to shrink away from his gaze.

"I have a headache," she admitted as she rubbed her temples. "It just happens sometimes."

Daniel nodded, staying silent instead of forcing her to keep talking. She leaned her head against the window of the car with her eyes closed, and he drove them back to the condo in silence.

Everything was louder and sharper. Her mind ran too fast and she couldn't focus.

Usually, her medicine would help her with this, but as she thought about it, she realized she hadn't taken it yet. It was hours after her usual dosage time.

No wonder she was struggling. *Damn it.* It was the first thing she needed to do when they got back to the condo.

They pulled in thirty minutes later, and Amelia barely waited for the car to be parked before she dashed upstairs. "Amelia?" John asked. "What are you—"

"Forgot my medicine. Daniel doesn't know about it, so zip it." The words rushed out of her, and she went to their room and took it as quickly as she could.

When she turned, she could see John's pursed lips, and she knew he definitely had something to say about Daniel not knowing about her ADHD.

But, thankfully, he kept his mouth shut.

Daniel walked into the condo, looking at her with concern.

"I just needed to take something for my head."

John's eyes widened at the lie, but she ignored him.

"O-okay," Daniel said. "But you can tell me if I did anything wrong. I can handle it."

John gestured to Daniel, eyes wide. She could read the message clear as day. *He's nice. Why aren't you telling him?*

But she'd never told him the real ways others had reacted to her ADHD. How even her best friend in college had mentioned the way the medications she took could be abused. How the one person she was supposed to trust the most completely betrayed her.

No. She couldn't do it again. Not for a real boyfriend, and especially not for a fake one.

"Mom said we were going to a taco shop for dinner," Amelia said. "Are you going?"

John rolled his eyes at her obvious aversion, but he didn't outwardly question it. "Maybe. Probably. Are you bowing out?"

"No, I'm fine. My—I mean, *the* medicine will do its work."

"You don't have to go if you don't feel up to it," Daniel added. "I could go and bring you something back."

"It's fine. We have a few hours and I'll be good by then."

It wasn't a lie. It was *possible* that she would be fine by then.

Just unlikely.

"I'll just go sit on the deck," she said. "Come find me if you need me."

She went outside, thinking the salty air would calm her nerves. It didn't. All she could think about was how Daniel had looked at her like she could explode at any moment.

And how she couldn't get her shit together long enough to make him believe she was fine.

She bit her tongue, hating that she hadn't kept it together as well as she'd wanted. This was why she was better off alone.

But slowly, she began to feel her medicine do its work. Sounds became less intense. She grew to enjoy the noise of the ocean again. But she felt like a bruise after the rough start to the day, and the guilt for not being normal lingered.

The door slid open and a glass of water appeared in her line of sight.

"Here," Daniel offered. "If you have a headache. This might help. I'm sure you don't want me to bother you, but I wanted to do something."

She slowly took the glass. *Damn it.* He was being so nice.

"Thank you," she replied. He turned to leave, and she realized she wasn't ready for that. "You could stay, if you wanted to."

He paused. "Are you sure?"

"I am." She moved over to give him more space. He scanned her face, as if looking for a lie. When he sat, she took it as a small win. "I'm sorry for acting weird. Target was . . . *a lot*."

"It was for me too."

"And I really did rush up here to take medicine," she added. "It's already helping."

"I know."

Her eyes traced over the tense line of his shoulders. "Are *you* okay?"

"I'm not going to bother you with my problems when you're not feeling well."

"I'm getting better," she reassured. "And besides, it would be nice to be out of my own head for a bit."

"It doesn't feel right."

"I'm asking. Please."

That seemed to do it. He let out a long sigh before speaking. "I guess when you weren't feeling well, I was nervous. Not because of anything you did, but because I was waiting for you to turn it on me."

"Wait, why would I turn my feelings on you?"

"Because I suggested going to Target? Because I didn't leave sooner? I don't know. But it feels like my fault somehow."

"It's not."

"Even if it's not, would it matter? It never did before."

"Oh," Amelia said. "Like with Lucinda."

"Yeah," he admitted quietly. "That's what life with her was like."

"That's not okay. My feelings are mine. Just like hers should have been her own."

"I know. Or I *should* know that. It got lost somewhere over the years of pretending like everything was fine."

She felt a pang of anxiety. "Daniel, I need to ask you something."

"What?"

"Does pretending with me bring up bad feelings? Am I somehow triggering anything?" She would feel like the worst kind of person if it did.

"Not all of it," he answered. "Some of it is completely different. You're not forcing me to be here or anything. But I don't know how you handle your bad emotions, and I'm used to how Lucinda handled hers, but that isn't your fault either."

It took the wind out of the beginning of a panic spiral. "I don't even want to have bad emotions, I just—"

"You're human. Why wouldn't you have them?" The words felt like a punch to the gut. "Besides, you're not yelling at me in private, so we're good."

"*Yell* at you? I would never. She sounds like a—" Amelia managed to stop herself for all of one second before the word came tumbling out. "—like a bitch."

He let out a chuckle. "You're right. But I *am* sorry about Target. And that I don't know how to be perfect for you."

"I don't need perfect. I'm definitely not that, so why would I expect you to be?"

"That's a very good point. You're pretty good at unraveling my thoughts."

That was funny because she could say the same thing about him. "I have a few talents." She gave him a smile.

He looked up, brown eyes meeting hers. "That's more like you."

Her heart skipped a beat at his words. It would be so easy to throw their pretense out the window and make this real, especially when he'd handled today so perfectly.

"We should go get ready," she said. "You're wearing white, and I doubt that's going to go well at a taco shop. This place is delicious but messy. You know what?" She eyed the unbuttoned shirt layered over his T-shirt. "Lose the top layer entirely. Go in just the T-shirt."

"Isn't that a little informal?"

"It's vacation, Daniel. And a taco shop. It's *all* informal. Come on. I'm doing you a favor here." She stepped closer. "If you take off this layer, you might be more comfortable."

Her hands came to rest on his shoulders. She was *supposed* to be anxious still, but her mind was moving far too fast for that. Now, it was solely focused on removing fabric from his firm shoulders.

Daniel looked down at her, one corner of his mouth raised. "The only way this shirt is coming off is if you take it off."

"I can work with those terms." She slid the fabric away from him. The button-down came off easily.

But it almost didn't feel like enough.

Daniel smiled, as if she'd done exactly what he'd wanted her to. Her heart pounded in her chest. If she leaned in just a few inches . .

.

"Ready for tacos?" John's voice was loud, breaking her out of her trance.

"Y-yeah," she said. "Always ready for tacos."

Maybe it was a good thing that her brother had interrupted. Because if he hadn't, then she might have made things far more complicated.

***

The thing about going to a live music night at a taco bar was that it was *loud*.

Amelia winced as they approached. Daniel put a hand on her arm, raising his eyebrow.

"Should we bail?" he asked, but she could barely hear him over the music.

Maybe she should have said yes, but she'd been feeling better after her medication kicked in. Maybe she would be fine.

She wished she was. She wished she was the kind of person who could do anything at any time and never get overwhelmed. It would make her life so much easier.

People were packed in, pushing Daniel and her close together. But his body against hers didn't feel as good as it should. It felt like she was trapped.

Her hands shook, but she kept them out of her sight. She didn't *want* to do this here. She didn't want to panic or overreact.

She was *fine*.

Her mind flashed to a scene from long ago. A party Andrew had taken her to. She'd been having a day like this, where she couldn't handle loud noises. He'd told her that she needed to buck up and deal with it.

And she told herself she could handle it. The night had ended in disaster. She'd found a room to hide out in, only for one of his friends to come in and hit on her. Andrew had been so mad. Not only that she had snuck away, but that she'd let someone else make a pass at her. It didn't matter that she hadn't wanted to be hit on.

It mattered that she hadn't been stuck to his side. It mattered that she got overwhelmed. According to him, every mistake could be traced back to that.

But this wasn't that night. She *knew* that. Yet every hand that brushed a part of her body felt foreign. It felt like that guy who couldn't take a hint.

Amelia's heart rate was through the roof. She couldn't breathe. She couldn't think.

She could see her family, and they were all fine. None of them were bothered. Not even Daniel was. He was heading for them, seemingly unaffected by it all.

Amelia tugged out of his grip. She couldn't go over there. It didn't matter that they were her safe people. She didn't want the questions. She didn't want *anyone* to look at her.

Daniel noticed it instantly. He turned, an eyebrow raised again. At his gaze, her mind flashed to Andrew's much crueler one.

And she ran.

As she did, a single word played over and over in her head.

Crazy.

"You're just crazy, Amelia!" Andrew had said many years ago. *"You're making things up, just like you always do! You're trying to throw me under the bus for your own problems."*

It didn't matter that she was running because she was back in her old apartment, dishes piled high as she tried and failed to keep up on chores. Andrew didn't help—his job was too demanding, and he wanted her to do it since she was only a full-time student. But she couldn't. No matter how hard she tried, no matter what vile words he called her, she just fell behind.

She couldn't handle it. She couldn't handle *anything*.

Why else would she freak out while driving, unlike literally everyone else she knew? Why else would she not be able to handle a perfectly normal evening at a taco shop? Why else would she fake an entire relationship?

Amelia felt like she was being attacked, but it was in her own mind. Her breaths came out ragged, as if she had run for miles and miles without a break.

She headed for the beach, which had plenty of seagrass to hide in. She was secure and *alone*. It was the perfect place for her panic.

Here, she didn't have to see her mother's eyes widen and look at her with pity or see the way her dad jumped in to try and fix it whenever she freaked out. She didn't want John's attempted kindness or Daniel's confusion on why she was upset.

She fell to her knees in the sand, her entire body shaking. Her face felt numb, like she couldn't gulp enough oxygen. Her old therapist would say she needed to deconstruct what she was freaking out about one piece at a time, but she couldn't. Not when every little thing was an opportunity to find panic.

"Amelia!" Daniel called. He was looking for her, but she mentally curled in on herself further, hoping he wouldn't find her hiding spot. She heard footsteps nearby, so close that he *had* to have seen her. But she couldn't look.

She couldn't even *look*.

A warm, solid hand lay gently on her back. She jumped as if it were the precursor to something much more painful.

It should have made it worse. She could easily find so many things to worry about if she thought hard enough.

But Daniel's hand felt different now that they were alone. The touch was enough to remind her that her thoughts weren't real. She wanted to berate herself for *needing* this, for doing this in the first place.

Those thoughts then passed her by, and for once, she wasn't dragged with them. They were like the current, always moving, yet she was planted in place.

Daniel's hand rubbed up and down her back. Eyes still fixed on the sand, she could see he had knelt beside her. She focused on every centimeter his hand moved and the warmth that radiated off his body. It felt like a life preserver.

She was finally able to focus on the world around her. She smelled the salty air, felt the cool, nighttime wind enveloping her, the grit of the sand beneath her, and Daniel's warm, calming presence. She heard families talking, kids screaming in the distance, the sound of the ocean washing over the sand and shells, taking it away into the dark night.

The anxiety that had a death grip on her went with the current too. She felt her body loosen. She blinked her eyes open and looked at the grains of sand underneath her. She noticed the grass half buried beside her and let out a long, slow breath.

She knew she needed to look at Daniel, but she still couldn't. The idea was terrifying, and she'd had enough panic for one day.

"I'm sorry." The words were low, and they weren't enough.

"You don't need to apologize," he said. "It's okay not to be fine."

"But I worried you."

"You're not responsible for my feelings."

Those were a version of *her* words, turned around on her like it was nothing. Amelia was used to Andrew twisting things, but never like this. She was used to being the one to bend. She would have the extra patience, extra kindness. Never them.

And she was not used to getting it in return.

"I overreacted. I know I did."

"Not really, considering you haven't been feeling well all day." His words were soft. Patient.

It made her throat close up. "It was loud."

"It was."

"I should have stayed home."

"Maybe. But that's in the past now. This is where we're at."

"Are you mad?"

"No, and it wouldn't matter if I was. I don't take my emotions out on people. And you don't need to take yours out on yourself, either."

"Wh-what?"

"If it were me, and I was with Lucinda, I'd know exactly how mad she was. And I'd do some of the work for her by being mad at *myself* for it. Does that sound fair?"

"No." Her eyes left the ground and she was *finally* able to look up at him. "I see your point."

"Good, because I wasn't sure I worded that right."

"It sounded dangerously close to what one of my therapists said, which is probably what I needed to hear."

"What else do they say?"

"To think about my surroundings, which I finally did. And to . . . stay home if I feel off."

"The closest thing to that is the condo. Should we go back?"

"I don't want to ruin your night."

"It's not ruined. Not if I'm with you."

"Are you sure?"

"I am *very* sure."

She huffed out a laugh. "I'm not entirely convinced you're real. Usually, people aren't this nice about my . . . panic."

"That's funny because I could say the same thing about you."

"We're two peas in a pod, I guess." This strange kinship prompted her to say even more. Things she never would say. "I have anxiety, by the way. I think a level-two boyfriend should know that."

It was a gamble. One that could end horribly.

But *God*, she didn't want it to. She stared at his features, waiting for the familiar judgment or an eye roll that she had received from so many others.

It didn't come.

"Level two? Have I been promoted?"

"On accident, but yes. You have."

"Then thank you for telling me."

"You have to have thoughts. Maybe questions."

"Only one."

"What is it?" Maybe it would be about her medication or how she even got her job.

"How do I help you with it?"

"What?" She had never been asked that before.

"I know at work you handle it remarkably well, but I want to be able to help you feel more comfortable. What can I do?"

"This," she said. "Just being here."

"Okay. Anything else?"

"I mean, that is *more* than enough."

"Not really. I consider being with you one of the easiest things I've ever done. And if that's all you need, then I'll happily do it. But if you ever need *more*, just ask."

Amelia blinked. She was so flabbergasted that she couldn't form words. Maybe he *wasn't* judgmental. Maybe he was like her parents.

But she felt a tug, a fear begging to be listened to.

Anxiety is easy. ADHD is not.

There were debates about medication. Debates about how it manifested in women. It required *nuance*.

"People would pay top dollar for this shit, Amelia," Andrew had said. *"And you're using it just to do what the rest of us can do easily."*

If Daniel questioned any of it, she might break. And she'd already done that tonight. Maybe it was best if she focused on answering his question and kept her other diagnosis to herself.

"The hand thing helped," she said. "And maybe tell me to stay home. Or that it's okay to."

Daniel nodded. "Okay," he said. "Then, in the vein of that, I think we should go back to the condo."

"Yeah. I definitely agree."

"You need some rest."

"I don't want to ruin your night," she repeated.

Daniel stood, brushing off his shorts. "I told you, it's not ruined if I'm with you."

Amelia could only look at him, wondering how she could ever go back to seeing him at work, all stiff and polished. Here, he had been himself, wearing casual clothes and letting his hair curl freely. He was an entirely different man than the one she thought she knew.

He held out his hand to her, offering her help to get up. She took it without hesitation, allowing him to pull her to her feet. His hand was warm and comforting, just as it had been on her back. She blinked at him for a moment, intensely grateful for his presence, before she pulled her hand out of his to brush the sand off of her own outfit and to pull her unruly hair back.

After she texted her family that she would have to skip the taco shop for the night, they made the short walk back to the condo.

When they got into their room, Amelia lay on the bed. All she wanted to do was sleep.

"I can go out on the balcony if you need alone time," Daniel said, pulling out a book from his bag. "I'll just be reading."

She usually would kill for alone time. When she was with Andrew, she always wanted to be away from him when she was upset. But the idea of being in this room and Daniel being somewhere else made an unknown emotion swell in her—one she didn't like.

She immediately knew she didn't want him to leave.

"Stay, please," she urged.

"Are you sure?"

She nodded.

"You're not just saying that for my sake?"

"I don't . . . I don't really want to be alone right now." She felt a blush rise to her face. "I understand if you do, but I kind of liked it when you were there with me."

The bed dipped with his weight.

"Okay, I'll stay."

"But you don't—"

"I'm fine with staying," he said. "It's a little dark to be reading outside anyway."

Amelia nodded, and he sat against the headboard, just barely touching her. She had room to move if she needed to, but she stayed rooted to the spot, enjoying his warmth.

For what felt like forever, she sat in silence. Usually, she would play on her phone, but she was so focused on being next to someone that she forgot to. She was lying down while he was sitting up, and if she moved just slightly, her head would be in his lap, which would be unbearably intimate.

"What are you reading?" she asked after a long moment of silence.

"It's a fantasy. It's one of my favorites, actually."

"What's it about?"

"Oh, you know, a kid in a bad environment being taken to a magical place where he can be himself," he replied. "It's a common trope, but . . ."

"It resonates with a lot of people," Amelia said. "Maybe I can read it sometime. It sounds really good."

"I could . . . read it to you now," he offered. Eyes wide, she looked up at him and found his face turning red. "Never mind, that was a weird suggestion—"

"No," she interrupted. "I'd love that."

"Here goes nothing," he muttered. "This is going to be mortifying if I'm a terrible out-loud reader."

But he wasn't. Hearing a world told through a voice she knew kept her engaged in a way most audiobooks couldn't. It didn't matter that he didn't start on chapter one. She was putting together pieces, hanging on to every one of his words.

She didn't want to fall asleep, even though she was exhausted. She clung to consciousness for longer than she should have, but eventually, she dozed off to the sound of his soft, low voice.

CHAPTER FOURTEEN

DANIEL

Amelia was out not long after he started reading. Daniel could tell she was tired, and he could only imagine what had been going through her head when she ran off. He could see her getting more and more tense as the day went on, but there had been nothing he could do about it.

He was relieved that she'd opened up at all. There had been so many nights when Lucinda was upset but shut him out, and they never talked about it. Eventually, he began doing the same, and she'd found someone else.

At least Amelia hadn't done that.

Thinking of his ex made him put down the book and rub his eyes. He never did any of this for Lucinda because he quickly learned that she would take advantage of it. But Amelia had fought to even accept help, despite the fact that she so obviously needed it. She had spent the trip making him comfortable, making sure he was having a good time. Of course, she would be exhausted.

He'd realized she was like him. She was willing to do things for others until she literally broke down. And he wasn't used to being around people who put others first.

He looked over at her calm form. Seeing her run off tonight was the moment he realized she'd taken a piece of him with her. He had to know she was okay. That was all that mattered.

As he gazed at her, he noticed the smooth curve of her cheek and full lips. He looked at her hair, wondering what it felt like.

Amelia adjusted herself and moved to lie on her other side, facing away from him. Focus broken, he realized that maybe he'd been looking at her for too long. He went to the kitchen to get a glass of water, his throat sore from reading out loud.

"You're up late," Randy said. Daniel jumped. He didn't know anyone else was awake. Randy held up his hands. "Sorry, kid. Didn't mean to scare you."

"It's fine," he replied. "I'm just lost in my own thoughts."

"Is Amelia okay?"

"I think so. She fell asleep as I was reading to her." His eyes fell to the floor. Maybe that was too much information.

But Randy smiled. "That's a good way to calm her down. Thank you for doing it."

Daniel blinked. "What? I thought you'd be . . ."

"Did you think I was going to get jealous or something that she has someone else treating her right? Nah, kid. The more the merrier. There's always room for love."

"Some dads are weird about it."

"Not me. If my daughter is opening up to someone, then that means she trusts them. And I trust her. After the last guy she dated . . . I know it doesn't come easy."

Daniel let out a breath that he hadn't realized he had been holding the whole trip. Randy patted his shoulder and settled onto the couch. He reached for the remote and turned on the TV. The silence was more comfortable, and it was nice to spend time with someone. It reminded Daniel of what he could have had with his own father, if only things could have been different.

"I don't blame her. For not trusting people, I mean."

Randy turned to him and smiled. "You're doing a good job of getting her to trust you. Mandy told me this was new, and even I could see that, but we're only a few days in. I wonder what'll happen by the end of the trip."

It was a terrifying idea, but it was also one he couldn't turn away from.

"I just didn't want her to be alone," Daniel said. "That's all it was."

"That's a good way to look at it." Randy nodded.

"Is that how you look at it?" Daniel asked, curious. Obviously, he and Mandy were doing something right if they'd been together this long.

"That's a part of it. Sometimes, everyone needs to be alone now and then, but I think Amelia has had enough of that."

"Me too."

"Sounds like you're two peas in a pod."

Daniel nodded but felt a lump in his throat. This was only temporary, he knew that. But hearing that Randy approved made him want to forget this was fake.

"Are you a fan of sports?" Randy asked, pointing to the TV. "We could probably catch a recording of a recent game."

Daniel panicked for a moment. Was this an invitation? Was Randy just being polite? Lucinda's dad had never done this before.

"Not really," Daniel replied. "But I can manage."

"Then what do you like?"

He considered it. "I don't have time to watch a lot of TV, but maybe . . . comedy? Something light?"

"I can work with that." Randy changed the channel to an old sitcom. "You can sit with me if you like," he offered. "It'd be nice to have some company since everyone else is asleep."

"Sure." Daniel sat next to him awkwardly.

They watched in silence, but Daniel found a sense of peace that he hadn't felt around his girlfriend's dad in . . . well, ever.

Fake girlfriend's dad, that is.

They caught the last few minutes of an episode, and it ended with the family all hugging each other after some major fight.

It must have inspired Randy to ask, "Tell me about your family, Daniel. Hopefully, they're like this."

He bristled. "Uh . . . My mom is great. She lives an hour and a half away from Atlanta. My sister is in Nashville."

"And your dad?"

Daniel only looked away.

"Sorry, kid," Randy said. "I don't wanna bring up bad memories. I'm just curious."

"It's fine. We're just . . . not close."

That was an understatement.

"Not everyone is," Randy said, sighing. "Actually, Amelia and John have never known Mandy's parents. They weren't what you would call supportive. So, it's okay not to be okay with who you came from."

"My dad recently did something pretty awful, and I don't think I want to forgive him for it," he admitted. He didn't know why he trusted Randy, but he desperately needed parental advice, and he sure as hell wasn't bringing his mom into this.

Randy hummed. "That's hard. Is anyone hurt?"

"Me," he replied.

"Then it's on you to forgive him, or not to."

"Not according to him." He muttered the words, mostly meaning them for himself, but Randy heard it. He raised an eyebrow, and Daniel sighed. "My dad thinks he can atone with God for anything he does, but not me."

"Well, that's a shame because we live on Earth with each other, not God," Randy said. "And if he's not apologized . . . hell, even if he did, you don't have to forgive everything to move on. It might help, but if you're not ready, it isn't gonna do anything."

"All my life, he's told me that because we're related, I should forgive him. This time included. He was the reason I got divorced and he's never apologized about it. He's never even shown any remorse. How can I look at him when I know he cares more about himself than me?"

"You can't, son. Some things are just unforgivable. You can try and let it go, but only for yourself. I know I don't have a right to say any of this, but from what I'm hearing, he's a shit father that got lucky with a good son, and you've outgrown him emotionally. The same thing happened to Mandy. Ultimately, it's easy to believe family always deserves forgiveness, but that's not right. We all deserve to be held accountable, family or not."

Daniel looked over at Randy and nodded. He had been working toward accepting that he wasn't going to be able to forgive his father and hearing someone else confirm it helped. Especially someone older and someone who was also a dad.

"Thank you," Daniel said. "I needed to hear that."

"I can tell. Now, enough about bad people who don't deserve our time. We've got another episode to watch."

CHAPTER FIFTEEN

AMELIA

When Amelia woke up, Daniel's arm was slung around her waist, and he was in a deep sleep. She felt an eerie sense of calm being in his arms. It would be so easy to stay here forever.

She got up, knowing that she didn't need to dream about things that wouldn't happen. Stepping into the bathroom, she changed clothes and ventured into the condo's living space, mind on coffee.

"Hey, honey," her mom said as Amelia was walking out of the bedroom. "Where are you going?"

"To get some coffee," she replied. "Do you want anything?"

"Mind if I go?"

"Are you feeling up to it?"

Her mom nodded. "I think I'm on the upswing. My medication is still working, even at the lower dose."

Amelia's eyes slid to the door, and she prayed Daniel was still asleep.

"Amelia, maybe I should ask—"

"Let's head out. We can talk on the way there."

She led her mother out the front door, eager to keep all medicine talk away from her significant other.

"You realize those medications mess with your brain, right?" Andrew used to say. *"Doesn't that scare you?"*

Daniel wasn't Andrew. She knew that, but she was still working on believing it.

"You're really not telling him anything?" her mother asked when they got to the elevator.

"He knows about the anxiety."

"But nothing else?"

Amelia slowly shook her head.

"Has he given you a reason not to tell him?"

"No."

"Really? You seem so adamant in keeping it quiet. Usually, people don't hide things without a reason."

The elevator doors opened and they headed toward the sidewalk. "He's a good guy. He's done nothing wrong."

"There is no other reason to hide it, unless Andrew was truly *that*—"

Amelia stopped walking. "Mom, can we not talk about this?"

"That's exactly what it is, isn't it?"

She pressed her lips together. Hearing Andrew's name almost sent her over the edge.

"Yes, Mom. That's exactly why." She turned around. "But before you ask why or what happened, just know that I *can't* talk about it. Yesterday was bad enough and I just want to enjoy the last few days of this vacation and not be stuck in the past."

"But how can I not ask questions when my daughter is hurting? It took you five years to even try with someone else."

More than that, considering this was all fake.

"I'm fine," she replied. "What happened with Andrew is over now. It just taught me what the real world is like. Now I know."

"But you know you're not . . . *broken* or anything, right? Your dad and I never wanted you to feel like you were."

"I know. It's others who see me that way. I'll tell Daniel if I feel like I need to, but for now, we're good."

"But if you trust him, then you should tell him."

"You don't have to fix my problems for me," Amelia said. "Just like you didn't before we went on this trip. Honestly, this reminds me of when I was a kid and you would have a manic episode."

Her mom sighed. "Yes. It's very similar to that. I've had mini ones since reducing my dosage, but I'm not as dizzy, so that's a bonus. I'm sorry. I know I was overbearing before, but I just want you to be happy."

"You don't worry about John like you do me. At least about relationships. You respect that he doesn't want one. So why not me?"

"Because you planned your wedding when you were four. You watched romantic comedies every day in high school. So when one day you said you were done with dating, I knew something bad had happened. And that something is still affecting you."

Amelia bit her lip. Her mom's observations were exactly right. She used to live for romance. She used to want a life partner and constantly daydreamed about her wedding.

And now, she couldn't think about it without getting sick.

"But . . . I'm getting too involved," she said. "I know that. I just miss the bright-eyed, hopeful Amelia."

"Me too," she muttered.

"My only hope is that you find someone who is as understanding for you as your dad is for me."

Amelia nodded. "We'll see. Tell me about your decrease in medication. I'd love to hear more."

Her mother accepted the change of topic easily enough, and Amelia was grateful. It was nice to hear why she'd needed an adjustment and how she was feeling now.

They got their drinks, plus one for Daniel. They went back up to the room and Amelia found that he had woken up and was freshly showered. He sat on the couch rather than sequestered in their room as he had for most of their trip.

"Hey," she greeted. "I got you a tea."

Daniel smiled. "I appreciate that. I could almost go for a coffee. I'm exhausted."

"How late were you up?"

"Way too late, but I can't seem to sleep in no matter what I do." Daniel took a sip of the tea.

"What made you stay up late?"

And was it her?

"Nothing major. I was up talking to your dad, actually."

"He said something about that," her mom said. "I tried to wake him up, but he muttered something about families in comedies."

"Yeah, we watched some TV too."

"Glad you two had fun," her mom said. "I think I'm going to try and wake him up again and go for a walk on the beach. Do you two have any plans for the day?"

"I was thinking about going to the pool," Daniel said.

"I'm up for that," Amelia replied. "It's early, so it shouldn't be too busy."

CHAPTER SIXTEEN

DANIEL

Out at the pool, Daniel's phone rang the moment he took off his shirt.

Amelia's eyes slid to his screen. "Is that . . . Lucinda?"

"Looks like it. I should probably take this, or else she'll keep trying." He grabbed the phone and stepped away, ignoring the feeling of Amelia's eyes following him.

"Why are you calling?" he asked in lieu of a greeting.

"Where are you? You're not home."

"Why are you at my apartment?"

"You never responded to the invite to the wedding," Lucinda said. "And *no* is not an acceptable answer."

"That's the answer you're getting. No, I will not come. And why are you at my apartment?" he repeated.

"Excuse me, *I* chose this place. If anything, it should have been mine."

"You got my dad's mansions all over the country. Why are you worried about an apartment that you agreed to let me have in our divorce?"

"It's not like you're using it. Where are you?"

Daniel rubbed a hand over his face, feeling a tension headache bloom in his temples. This was like the night before the trip when she'd come over unannounced. She was trying to stir up some sort of emotion from him, but he didn't feel a single thing toward her.

Except annoyance.

"I'm on vacation," he said.

"What? Since when do you go on vacations?"

"Since my girlfriend invited me on one."

"Oh, the girlfriend? That's right. I heard about her. What is she—a rebound? I bet she's not even prettier than me."

"Lucinda," he ground out.

"Come on, you can admit it."

"The only thing I can admit is that you are a thorn in my side. You divorced me, Lucinda. That means you leave me alone."

"We're never done, sweetie. I'll always have a piece of you."

"You never had any of me from the start," he snapped. "You were the worst mistake I ever made. I don't want you. I don't care about you. We are done, and I am with a woman who is *nothing* like you and I love every second of it."

"Nothing like me? What does that mean?"

"It means she's not a manipulative bitch like you are. I'm done talking to you. Goodbye."

He hung up and then turned his phone to silent. This was how all of their arguments used to go. Lucinda would push and push and then get mad if he said what he truly felt.

"Wow," a voice said. "You said everything I thought about her."

He turned, eyes wide at the sight of Amelia.

"You weren't supposed to hear that."

"Why not? It was kind of awesome."

"I don't like being angry."

"Considering what I've heard she's done, I think she deserved it. Why did she call anyway?"

"To try and force me to go to her wedding to someone else."

"Manipulative bitch was the correct terminology," she replied. "And I'm sorry I followed you. I wanted to be here in case it was a bad conversation, or if you decided to take her back."

"That's not happening. *Ever*."

"I didn't think so, but sometimes my anxiety tells me wild things. I'm sorry she ambushed you with that."

"It was hardly the worst thing she's done."

"So, she's engaged already? To who?"

His stomach sank at the question, but soon, she'd know anyway.

"My father."

Amelia blinked. "I'm sorry. *What?*"

"She left me for my father."

"Your—Oh, holy *shit*. That's awful."

"It is, but she wanted a rich husband who dotes on her and my father is that. They're going to go public with it when we get back."

"Public with it?"

"He's famous. Once he tells people, everyone will know."

"What does he do? Please tell me he doesn't own our company."

Daniel shook his head. "God, no. Have you heard of Michael Anderson?"

"The preacher?"

He nodded.

"*Him?* That's your dad?"

"Yes."

Amelia stared at him as if taking in his features to see if he was lying. "I can kind of see it, but also not really. Daniel, that's horrible."

"That he's my father or that my wife left me for him?"

"Both," she said. "How are you even functioning?"

"Because her leaving was a bit of a blessing. And I also know she doesn't love him. She wants the money. And to hurt me."

"Oh, is that all? I'm glad I took her off the approved visitors list at work. Wait, this is why you want to pretend at the office, isn't it?"

He nodded. "It's going to be huge news when the story drops. I'm going to look horrible."

"Hang on, you know it doesn't make *you* look bad, right?"

"She left me for my father, Amelia. I don't see how this *doesn't* look bad for me."

"It looks bad on *her*. She left you, not for someone that's her age, has a regular job, and is kind and loving. She left you for someone who is *rich*. That's not what normal people do."

"I know . . . but it's still embarrassing."

Amelia's face turned soft. "I understand that. I would feel that way too. But it's not your fault."

"I'm not blameless in all of this either."

She frowned. "Why not?"

He sighed. "I wasn't a very good husband. I mean, I tried to love her in the beginning, but she always wanted me working or making money, and then I just started focusing on that and less on her."

"That doesn't mean she can cheat on you, though."

"In my father's eyes, that's why it's okay that she did. And some-times . . . I believe him. I wasn't great to her in the end because I just shut down. I barely talked to her and I was never home. So, it almost makes sense why she would want to leave."

"But why did you shut down?" she asked. "There has to be a reason."

He took a moment to think about it. "Because she only cared about how she looked to the world. We would go on a hike and none of it would be spent hiking, just posing for the perfect picture. Or when we got our apartment, she wanted it to look perfect, and I never got a say in it. I felt like I was just the person funding the life she wanted. But there was nothing else there."

"You ran yourself until you shut down. Kind of like I did last night."

Daniel sighed. "Yeah, that's exactly what I did."

"And when that happened to me, you were there for me. But when you did that to her, she left. And that's wrong. We all get tired.

Maybe not as intensely as I did, or as you did, but it should be a two-way street. What did she do for you that helped you?"

"I . . . I can't think of anything."

Amelia waved her hand, as if it absolved everything. "You weren't happy. Why didn't you leave?"

"I don't think I knew I had the option. I mean, obviously, I wasn't happy, but it *looked* like I was, and I was pretending that I was, so I thought I had no reason to feel like I did and that I was actually happy."

"I get that, but you definitely did have a reason. I'm sorry that happened."

He looked down. "I just have to get through this reveal that they're planning, and then . . . I don't know. I don't think I can ever marry someone again if it ends up this way."

"You know, not everyone is going to be like her," she said softly. "It's entirely possible you could find someone else and actually *be* happy."

He looked at her. He wasn't blind to his own feelings. He knew that *she* could easily be someone he could move on with.

But he doubted she wanted that in return. She'd made it clear that she was happy being alone. She didn't need a partner, not in the way he was starting to see her.

"Yeah, maybe."

"Don't rush it. I mean, I'm going on year five of getting over someone, so take your time."

Daniel wished she'd never had the ex that turned her away from love. He wished he had met her first.

"Do you want to go to the beach?" he asked. "I don't think I can take thinking about it too much longer."

"Sure," she said, smiling. "I'm always up for a little distraction."

She led him to the beach where he completely forgot about the phone call as they treaded into the surf.

The waves were taller than usual; they dumped cold water on them from the moment they got to waist level.

"This is *freezing*!" she yelped.

"I thought you liked to jump right in."

"Not today I don't." She shrieked as another hit her, wetting her entire back. Daniel couldn't help but laugh as half of her hair got wet.

He had turned his back on the waves—a rookie mistake. A wave crashed over him, soaking him far more than Amelia.

"That's what you get," she said, finally dropping her whole body in the water. "It's rude to laugh at your girlfriend."

"Not when she's funny," he replied. He shook the excess water out of his hair.

"Ooh, this is a good one," she said, eying a tall wave heading their way. "Think I can ride this all the way back to the shore?"

"You can try."

She dove into the water, swimming ahead of the wave. He plunged under it, knowing he couldn't jump. When he resurfaced, Amelia was gone. A few seconds later, she appeared at the shore.

"I swallowed so much sand!" she called. "But that was awesome!"

"Think you can teach me?"

"You have to be ready to be beaten up by a wave," she said as she slowly made her way back to him. "Can you handle it?"

"I'm willing to try anything once."

It was not as easy as Amelia had made it look. There was an art to hitting the wave at the perfect moment to be carried to the shore. It took him many attempts, but after a dozen wipeouts, he could finally feel the water surge around him as a wave sent him all the way to the shore.

She wasn't kidding when she said he needed to prepare to be beaten up. Sand got everywhere, and there was a moment where he didn't know what direction was up. But then he surfaced, and he could feel the rush of adrenaline.

"We did it!" Amelia cheered. She was on her knees, having landed that way after the ocean spit her out. Her hair was splayed over her face, and she was somehow covered in more sand than him. Despite the back-to-back failures, it was the most fun he'd had in a while.

"It was, though I think I might need some not-salt water. I swallowed more than the recommended amount."

She slowly stood. "I'll go with you. I should probably drink some too."

There was a vendor selling drinks out of a cooler. Daniel paid an exorbitant amount for two bottles of water, but he didn't regret it. He needed hydration. He drank half of the bottle, and when he was finally done, he looked over and saw she had completely finished hers.

"Good call on the water," she said, out of breath. "I needed that. I feel like an old beater car with all of its warning lights on."

"Let me guess, you're hungry too?"

"How did you know?"

"Because I'm starving."

"I'll get us food. And before you offer, you paid an arm and a leg for this water, so I'll get lunch. There's a sandwich place not too far from here."

"Are you—"

"Yes!" She was already grabbing her cover-up. "I'll be back in a few."

She was gone before he could ask again. She was *fast* when she was determined to get something done.

Daniel found a table by the pool deck, content to watch the people walk by.

Families played in the water with smiles on their faces. It was relaxing to slow down and not look at his phone. Maybe he needed to do this more often.

"Daniel? Is that you?"

He looked over and saw that Mandy had walked up. She had a book in hand. "Hi," he replied. He hadn't talked to her much, save for their one coffee shop visit at the beginning of the trip, and he knew she hadn't been feeling well.

"What are you up to down here?"

"Amelia and I were swimming and she just left for lunch."

"Good. I was hoping you two were having a good time. Mind if I sit for a bit?"

"Go ahead," he said.

"I'm sorry I haven't been feeling well. I know it can be frustrating when one person isn't participating."

"It's not frustrating at all. I'd rather you take care of yourself."

"That's very sweet of you. Though nothing is physically wrong. It was up here." She pointed to her mind.

Daniel nodded. "It's all the same to me."

Mandy smiled. "Really? That's good to hear."

"It's basic decency. The brain is a part of the human body too."

"You'd be surprised at how many people disagree," she replied. "But enough about me. How are *you* enjoying yourself?"

"It's been fun. I haven't been on a vacation in a very long time. And even when I had, I found reasons to work." He shook his head. "But this time, I'm enjoying myself. Amelia just taught me how to bodysurf. I've never been that covered in sand, yet it was the most fun I've had in a while."

"She got someone else to do it with her? That's fabulous. She loves swimming in the ocean with others, but it's never been John's thing. He hates all the sand."

He gave a little shrug. "I'll deal with it if I'm having fun."

"And if you ever . . . you know, *want* to take Amelia out on a date, there are a few things you can take her to do in Charleston that she would *love*." Mandy winked.

It would look bad to say no. That had to be the only reason he leaned forward and said, "Tell me. I'd love to take her out on a date."

And Mandy did. He committed them all to memory, wondering if he could get away with taking her to them as a friend and nothing more.

But then he wondered if *he* would be okay with going as her friend and nothing more.

"I'm back!" Amelia announced as Mandy whispered one last option to him. "I didn't know if you wanted sauce or no sauce or if you wanted chips or fries, so I got both. And two kinds of sandwiches. And more water."

"I'm sure whatever you've picked out for me will be fine," he said. "I'm not very picky."

"Okay, good because—" Amelia paused when she finally noticed Mandy. "Mom? Were you there the whole time?"

"I was, but I didn't want to interrupt. Besides, I got my time to talk to Daniel." She winked again and stood. "You two enjoy lunch."

"Why do I feel like she just planned something?" Amelia eyed Mandy as she walked away.

"We really just talked," he replied. "And she gave me some ideas."

"Ideas for what?"

"A date. For us."

"A *date*?" she asked. "What kind of date?"

"I think that would be breaking the boyfriend code if I told you."

"The fake boyfriend code says otherwise."

"But in her eyes, it's real, and it would be a letdown if I told you ahead of time."

"You're good at this," she said. "So, you're taking me on a date?"

"If you want. We don't have plans tonight and . . ." He trailed off, trying to come up with a reason other than he *wanted* to take her out. "It would look good?"

"It would," she said, biting her lip. "But still, no one would be around."

"And we would just be hanging out. Sure, some of the ideas were kind of romantic, but we're both adults. We can be mature about it."

"Fine. You've convinced me."

"Should it be this hard for a level-two boyfriend to convince you to go on a date?"

"Careful. Or I'll demote you."

"Message received."

"Though I might feel better after I eat."

CHAPTER SEVENTEEN

AMELIA

Amelia couldn't sit still on the car ride over. She didn't have an excuse—she had taken her medication, but the idea of Daniel taking her out on a date had her mind racing. What if he hadn't learned anything yesterday and he took her to something loud and unruly?

Or worse, what if he *did* learn something from the day before, and he was planning the perfect date?

She didn't know which she wanted. Her heart was in a dangerous position, and she might just lose her grip on things if today went perfectly.

They were driving to Charleston, that much was for sure. Amelia had always loved the city but never wanted to make the drive out here by herself. A few times, John had gone with her, but he had an amazing talent for finding partners to go home with and she usually found herself driving back alone.

"Are you going to tell me any part of your plan?" she asked. "And why we had to leave right after we got changed?"

"Fine. I'll tell you a part of it. The Angel Oak Park closes at five."

She eyed the time. It was almost four. "You're taking me to see the Angel Oak tree?"

"I am."

"That's one of the few places I haven't been to. Did my mom tell you about this?"

"She mentioned a tree but not a specific one," he replied. He was right. She'd always wanted to see it, but her family usually packed vacations with other sightseeing opportunities, and she couldn't ever convince them that an old tree was interesting, even if it was historical. "But I could have gotten it wrong. We could do something else."

"No!" she said quickly. "I've always wanted to go. Thank you for picking it out."

"Good. Then I got one thing right."

She had a feeling he was going to get many things right.

By the time they parked, Amelia was buzzing with anticipation. The tree was massive, far larger than the photos made it look. She found herself trailing the branches with her eyes, wondering just how something could grow so large.

"There's so much shade," she said. "Isn't this incredible?"

"It is. Do you want me to get a photo of you with it?"

She nodded. She spent a minute getting into position. Daniel snapped a few pictures.

He was putting his phone away when someone nearby asked, "Do you want some of the two of you?"

"Yes," Amelia replied before she could stop herself. "That would be great." She gestured for Daniel to walk over and pulled him close.

"Such a cute couple," the person said. "There you go. I got a few."

"Thanks!" Amelia said as Daniel grabbed his phone.

"You didn't have to include me," he said.

"We need photos for if my mom asks." She knew it wasn't the full truth. She wanted the photos to remember this.

To remember *him*.

"Let's walk around more," he suggested. "I think I saw a gift shop as we were walking in."

The summer heat wasn't as intense under the shade, so they were able to gaze at the massive branches for a while before they needed to find cooler air. Amelia bought a mug that she didn't need, but she wanted other items to help her remember this moment.

"Okay, what's next on your date master plan?" Amelia asked as they walked back to her car.

"Now we go on a walk."

He drove her to Hampton Park, a place she'd only been to once. John was more of a fan of the nightlife, and she'd had to drag him kicking and screaming to see the park. She'd loved it, with its ponds, oak trees, and colorful floral arrangements. John had been bored out of his mind.

The colors were different this year, with new annual flowers planted. It was still a warm day, and she could hear cicadas singing their tune in the trees.

"I figured we could do a lap or two."

"Yes," she said, grabbing Daniel by the arm and dragging him to the pathways. She took her time to admire all of the hues of the flowers and all the ducks in the water. It was warm enough to keep the crowds away. It didn't take long for her to put her hair up in a bun, but the scenery made her willing to tolerate the heat.

By the time they'd done a lap, though, she was dying for something to drink.

Daniel seemed to read her mind. "There is a coffee shop down the road," he said. "Let's go get something to cool off."

She eyed the sweat on his forehead, wondering why he'd dealt with the heat for so long. Luckily, the shop wasn't far, and they were able to find something to cool them off. The small shop was crowded with people looking to find a caffeinated oasis in the heat, but Amelia didn't mind settling close to him as she waited.

"This is the greatest thing I've ever had," she said, lifting her iced latte.

"The smoothie isn't bad either," he replied.

"Thank you for taking me to the park. This was a great date."

"Do you really think it's over already? I'm not done with you yet."

The words sent a shiver down her spine. "R-really? What else is there to do?"

"We haven't even had dinner," he said. "Now, would you like seafood or would you like nice scenery?"

"You mean I get to choose?"

"I have a feeling that will make tonight much more enjoyable. Which one will it be?"

"But what about what *you* want?"

"I will be perfectly happy at either."

Damn. That was such a good answer that she couldn't do anything but answer truthfully.

"I want nice scenery."

"Okay, then. Nice scenery it is."

The restaurant was the loudest part of the evening, but Daniel found a beautiful eatery inside an old church, so she couldn't complain.

"I've heard of this place," she said, eyes tracing over the stained-glass windows. "I've never been, though."

"Just like the oak tree, the photos don't do it justice."

"Definitely not. I don't even know if I need the food." Her stomach growled angrily. "Scratch that. I *do* need the food."

Daniel smiled at her, his full grin making her heart skip a beat. She didn't see him smile like this in the office, and it made her wonder if this was only for her.

"I hear the food here is good too," he said.

She had to tear her eyes away and force herself to look at the menu. Despite her hunger, she didn't care to pick out her meal. She'd rather either look at the man across from her all night or the beautiful colors of the stained glass in the restaurant.

There was a new kind of heat within her, and it had nothing to do with the temperature outside. She'd felt it in the hot tub too. She *wanted* him. She always had, but getting to know him made it all worse.

What would he be like in bed? Would he be as attentive and caring as he'd been for the whole trip? Would he whisper soft words to her while his hands caressed her most delicate areas?

"—do you think, Amelia?"

"Huh?" she blurted out. "Sorry. I was lost in space."

"It's fine," he said. "I was asking if you wanted queso. I was thinking about getting it for us."

That was the hottest thing he could have said.

"If there is ever a question about getting queso," she said, "the answer is always yes."

"Noted. I'll get the large."

Their food came out quickly and Amelia didn't remember eating a single bite of it. She was far hungrier than she thought she was, especially after their stroll through the parks. She was done with her food long before Daniel was, but he seemed content to listen to her ramble about her last few vacations with her family while he finished eating.

"This was great," she said as he paid the check. "You're definitely going above and beyond as a fake boyfriend."

"We have one more place to go," he said. "If you're up for it."

"We saw two of the most beautiful parks in Charleston, plus had a fancy dinner. What else could there be?"

"Dessert. And it's on the way back to the condo."

"That is tempting," she said. "Fine. I'll take you up on it."

She expected Daniel to find an artisanal dessert parlor nearby. Charleston was filled with those, but their destination took them farther inland than she was expecting.

"Wait a second," she said. "I know this place."

"Really? How odd."

They pulled into a diner and ice cream parlor, one that Amelia had spent many hours in. Her family had often stayed in Charleston before discovering the condo, and because she had been too young to remember the name of the shop, the details of it faded into the background when their new summer vacation location became Folly Beach.

Its importance to her had faded away too, until now, when Daniel brought it back into her life.

"How did you . . .?"

"I can't take all the credit. Your mom told me there was a diner-style ice cream shop that you loved. I hoped I picked the right one."

"This is the *exact* place."

"It's the only one that's been open long enough for you to come to."

"Are you calling me old?"

"Kind of. Twenty-eight years can be a long time."

She couldn't even be mad. All she could do was look at the place that was long since forgotten.

"Do you want to go in?" he asked after a moment. "We could wait if you wanted to."

"No," she said. "I'm definitely ready to go in."

From the moment she walked in, she was hit with a wave of nostalgia that made her eyes water. They used the same menus, had the same decor, and even had the same gumball machines that she remembered.

"I've gotta get a banana split," she said. "They still have it."

This place was more crowded than the restaurant, but she was determined to get her prize. Daniel got in line behind her, eyes on the menu. A few kids ran past, making Amelia shuffle closer to him to let them through.

He didn't even look down, but his arm wrapped around her, pulling her tighter.

She knew the position was better. Her being so close to him made a larger walkway for anyone who needed to get to the napkins or trash can on the wall.

But this wasn't a *real* date. "I-I should maybe move."

He finally looked down at her, and she could have melted in his gaze. "I think you should stay right here. Being this close seems perfect on a date."

"Even a fake one?"

"I'm fine with it if you are."

And she was. She knew she wouldn't dare to move away from him. Being next to Daniel like this was becoming her favorite place to be.

They stayed close until they ordered their ice cream. Once she had her sugary treat in hand, it was all she could focus on. She hadn't had a banana split like this in far too long.

"Thank you for this night," she said as they walked to the car. "It was amazing."

"I'm glad. I enjoyed it too. More than you know." His eyes lingered on her face, and she could have sworn she saw his gaze slip to her lips.

"W-we should head back. It's getting late."

He nodded, going around to the driver's side to get them home. Amelia felt her shoulders sag, but not with relief.

Daniel hadn't kissed her. That should have been a good thing. It meant their relationship was still fake and they hadn't crossed any lines.

But she wasn't happy with that. She wanted more. And now that she'd imagined what his lips could feel like on hers, she wanted to experience it. She couldn't get her mind off of it, even though she tried.

It was only a thirty-minute drive back, and the whole time, she turned over every moment of their date in her mind, wondering how it could have ended differently. Every moment of it had been perfect, up until she'd put the brakes on things.

They pulled in to the parking lot. Amelia wrestled with her own guilt and got out of the car. She glanced up at the condo, only to see someone poking their head out the front door.

She paused. "My mom's watching for us."

"I suppose she is," Daniel replied. "I hope this isn't the part of the date where she lectures me for bringing her daughter home past curfew."

"Or the awkward part where you drop me off at the door."

"I certainly hope not. I'd have to get a hotel room if I did." He gave her one last smile before brushing past her to go toward the door.

"Wait," she said. "I know this isn't *exactly* like when you'd drop me off at the door. But technically, we're supposed to be dating. And *if* that was a real date, then it was a great one, and I think I'd owe you a kiss at the end of it."

He blinked, jaw agape.

"Or," she continued after seeing his reaction, "we can just forget I ever said that and go inside."

"I don't think I can," he said.

"I'm sorry. I made it awkward."

"No, you didn't. *I* made it awkward because I'm standing here like an idiot when I have a woman like you offering to kiss me."

"It's only fair. It's what I would do if . . ." She trailed off. She wanted to do it with no ifs, ands, or buts. She had no idea how to explain it, though. So, instead, she stepped close, looking up to meet his eyes. "Is that a yes?"

Daniel didn't use words. Instead, he leaned down to press his lips against hers. It was soft, barely explorative, and it wasn't enough.

That mere brush of lips awoke something in her, and she needed more. More pressure. More time. More *everything*.

Amelia's hand wrapped around his neck, and she pressed herself into him harder. She could feel his sharp intake of breath, and she only had half a second to wonder if she was taking it too far before he pushed her against the side of her car.

This was a side of him she'd never seen. He was always quiet and calm, but this . . . this was the hottest thing she'd ever experienced. His teeth nipped at her bottom lip, soon followed by his tongue.

And she quickly realized that he was not only unfairly attractive. He was also a damn good kisser too.

Amelia opened her mouth to him, feeling his tongue brush against hers. He took up every inch of her mind, allowing nothing else to break through.

And then her car alarm went off.

They sprung apart, Daniel reacting quicker than she did. He fumbled with the keys and hit the lock button, silencing the loudness.

It gave her a second to think about what she'd done and realize that they'd just blasted past a boundary that she wasn't sure was supposed to be broken. She looked at his kiss-swollen lips and wondered if they would ever be the same.

"You know what?" she started. "I think we made our point."

"Definitely."

"And we're good, right? We're not . . . going to make this weird?"

"Not at all."

She nodded, grateful that his mind seemed to be right where hers was.

"We should head to bed. I bet we're tired."

"Very."

She rushed up the stairs. She told herself that she wasn't going to think about that kiss any longer. It was over, and besides, it was only for show.

But she was lying to herself.

***

The next morning, Amelia was very much replaying that kiss in her head when she woke up in Daniel's arms again.

They hadn't even gone to sleep near each other. She'd folded herself on the very edge of her side of the bed, and he'd followed suit.

But apparently, they didn't continue that trend when asleep.

Being near him felt like a new normal, one that she knew would end badly. Rationally, she knew they hadn't talked about what to do if they found themselves feeling anything for each other. He didn't know everything about her mental health, and she didn't know if he was even ready to move on after Lucinda.

And yet, those reasons did *nothing* to quell her desire for him. His body was hard against hers, and she couldn't help but notice one part of his body was harder than the rest.

She bit her lip, and her brain imagined exactly what that hardness could do to her. It was easy to imagine him sliding into her, filling her in a way she hadn't been in far too long.

All of her logic flew out the window and her hips jerked back, eager to feel even more of him.

Daniel's arm around her tightened, pulling her impossibly closer.

"What are you doing to me?" His voice was rough and low. Her skin broke out into goose bumps.

"I-I could ask you the same thing."

His grip went slack and he pulled away. "You're awake?" he asked.

She missed his warmth, but her brain was slowly coming back online. He'd done the right thing by pulling away. She knew that.

But she was disappointed.

"I need to shower," he said. "Sorry about . . . that."

"It's fine. It was bound to happen."

"Still. I wasn't thinking." He got up before she could say anything else. She let out a groan. What would have happened if she'd just kept her mouth shut? Would he have gone further?

And did she want him to?

She got up and went to get a glass of water and take her medicine. She needed to be in top mental condition *not* to climb him like a tree.

But she was beginning to wonder if she'd do it anyway.

"So, how was your date?"

She jumped and nearly choked on her water. "Mom! Don't sneak up on me like that."

"Sorry. I just had to ask. You guys were gone almost all night." She winked.

"You know, sometimes it's weird that you're not more protective," she said as she put her pill bottle back into her purse.

"You're a grown woman, and I'm happy for you, honey. This was what I wanted for you all along."

Amelia gritted her teeth. Everything was so *complicated* right now. She didn't know how to share in her mom's excitement over anything.

"Thanks," she said.

"Is everything okay?"

"You know me." She shrugged, trying to shake off her bad mood. "I'm not my usual happy self before coffee."

"I'd say let's fix that, but we're out of the free stuff. And we're only here a little longer, so buying more isn't worth it."

"It's fine," Amelia said. "I'll survive."

"So, how was the date?" her mom repeated. "What did you do?"

"We mostly did what you told him I liked. We went to the Angel Oak tree, and then to Hampton Park, and this beautiful restaurant in an old church—"

"Hold on. You did *all* of those things? I only told him about one of the pretty trees and ice cream."

"Yeah, we did all of that." Her cheeks burned.

"Did you enjoy it?"

"Of course I did. It was a perfect date. He even found the ice cream shop we went to when I was little."

"He did?" Her mom smiled. "Oh, I was hoping it was still open. He has some good detective skills."

"He's smart."

Almost too smart for me. The thought hit her like a truck, and she looked down at her feet.

Her mother caught it. "Oh, honey, don't get into your own head. You two are adorable."

"Right," she said. "I'm sure we are."

"I think this is the start of something great. Is it too soon to invite him back next year?"

"Mom, I haven't even told him about . . ." She eyed the door to their room down the hallway. "You know."

"Something tells me he is going to handle it as perfectly as always."

"I don't know if that's true."

"Don't let exes spoil someone better. What's in the past is over now."

Was it over when she kept reliving it every time someone was mad at her? It seemed like it would follow her forever.

The door to their room opened and Daniel stepped out, freshly showered. He looked good in his simple T-shirt and jeans.

"Morning," her mom said, smiling over at him. "Do you two have plans this morning?"

"Not really," he replied. "Why?"

"We should all go out for breakfast. John and Randy are on a walk, so I have nothing else to do."

Daniel looked at Amelia, but it was almost difficult to meet his eyes after what had happened just a few minutes ago.

"I'm fine with it," Amelia said. Maybe her mom could be a buffer for them.

"That's fine." He added, "I'm starving."

"Do you mind if we take your car?" her mom asked.

"Yeah, of course."

"Do you have your keys?"

"I've delegated them to my driver." She pointed at Daniel. "So far, they've never been lost."

"We had one issue with the car alarm, but that wasn't my fault."

Amelia nearly gave herself whiplash turning to him, but he was smiling. "It was a group effort," she replied, chest loosening at the joke. If he was joking, then hopefully, they were okay—not lost in a pit of their own awkwardness.

Her mom had a restaurant in mind, and she usually had good taste. They got there before the breakfast rush and were seated immediately. The waitress asked for their drinks, and everyone got water, plus Amelia asked for a cup of coffee.

"Yay, life juice!"

"I would think water is life juice," Daniel remarked.

"Not for me. I'd be so happy if I could live off of only caffeine."

He raised an eyebrow and scooted her water cup closer to her. "Until you remember you're thirsty," he said. "I seem to recall you downing and entire water bottle in one go yesterday."

"How dare you call me out on that." But she took a sip of water anyway.

"I'm so glad I'm feeling better," her mom said. "I would have missed seeing this!"

"I'm glad you are too," he added.

Amelia looked between the two of them, biting her lip. Hopefully, this didn't go where it seemed to be going.

"The medication I'm on still helps. I can have things like coffee without getting nauseous." She lifted her hands up in celebration.

Amelia's eyes were wide. That was *exactly* what she didn't want to happen.

But Daniel didn't treat it like it was a big deal.

"It's good that you found that balance. My sister-in-law was on too high of a dose of an antidepressant after their adoption was finalized, and she said she felt numb. She was much more like herself when she lowered it."

"I didn't know you knew much about medication, but it's good you're so understanding." Her mom looked at Amelia with an arched brow.

See? her mother seemed to be saying. *Nothing to worry about.*

"I don't know the details, but I know it helps her, and that's what matters."

"What a great way to look at it." Her mom's eyes were still on Amelia, whose body felt like it was on fire.

So, Daniel was okay with medication. He was okay with . . . a lot. Slowly, all of her reasons for not wanting a relationship were being disproven.

Yet, she was still terrified to ever bring it up herself. If it was right, shouldn't she not be scared? Her radar had gotten much better over the years, and this fear had to be a bad feeling about him manifesting.

He probably wouldn't like it if his *girlfriend* had it. That was it. A sister-in-law was a much more distant connection.

"They have banana split waffles, Amelia," Daniel said. "That might be up your alley."

"Uh . . . yeah," she said, shaking herself out of her thoughts. "Maybe."

The waitress interrupted to ask for their food order, and Amelia got Daniel's suggestion. Once she left, her mom and Daniel talked for the whole breakfast. She seemed to be dying to know anything and everything about him, and he seemed willing to share it. She was over the moon when they discovered they liked the same book series and spent half an hour dissecting it like an English teacher with Shakespeare.

Amelia could only sit back and watch. Andrew and her mom had *never* gotten along like this.

They got back to the condo around midday, and they were *still* talking. Amelia didn't mind—she was glad not to have to field conversations between the two of them. Eventually, her mom went to spend some time with her dad, and John mentioned he was going to be hanging out with someone, which just left Daniel and Amelia.

"Looks like you and my mom hit it off," she said after everyone had left.

"We did," he said with a smile. "She's a great mom. She reminds me of mine."

"You reacted really well about the medication talk too."

"Did I?" he asked. "I was just being a decent person. Needing medication for mental illness isn't the end of the world."

"Well . . . to some people it is."

"Not to me. Lots of people under me have asked for accommodations and I always give them what I can. People are people, even if they need help."

That was a good response.

It would be so easy to tell him then. She could just let it slip out and say that she had something too. Then it would be over and she would be free.

But she couldn't. No matter how hard she tried. The words wouldn't come out. All she could hear was Andrew's mocking laugh.

"So, do you have any ideas on what to do today?" she asked instead. Instantly, her cheeks heated with shame. Why couldn't she do this?

"How do you feel about being out in the heat?"

"I can tolerate it if I'm having fun. Why?"

"This is going to sound so lame, but there are so many mini golf courses around here."

Her eyes lit up. "And you want to go?"

"I do."

"Yes! No one ever wants to go with me around here. Plus, it's a bit of a drive to the nearest one."

"I don't mind a drive. Why don't the others want to go with you?" he asked.

"I might be competitive about it. I don't know if you can handle it."

"It depends on if I win or not."

"Are you challenging me?"

"I think I am."

"Then we're going," she said, practically pushing him out the door, all thoughts of her ADHD forgotten.

No one was at the mini golf course since it was so hot. They both got a discounted rate, and each got a card to keep track of the other's score. They had chosen a multiple-level golf course that was both challenging and fun.

Amelia loved mini golf, and it was absolutely thrilling that Daniel did too. They kept neck and neck throughout the entire game, teasing each other lightheartedly if one of them messed up and groaning when the other would pull ahead.

He won by one point and she was beyond upset about it.

"We're having a rematch," she told him as they walked to the car. The sun was setting and people were beginning to line up at the course. "You and me, before we leave."

"You're on," he agreed. "But I'm pretty sure I'll win that one too."

"No, you just got lucky on that one hill I couldn't make."

"That wasn't luck. It was skill."

"You're full of shit."

"We'll see with the rematch." Amelia rolled her eyes and went to the passenger's side to climb in. Daniel drove back to the condo, still gloating about his victory. When they got back, they went to the room only for a few minutes, until deciding to go swimming.

She knew she needed to keep herself busy because if she didn't, it was entirely possible she would either kiss Daniel again or spill all of her secrets. Neither were good options. No one was around to keep her in check, and as they spent more time together, she gravitated toward him more and more.

There was a wild group of kids at the pool, so they got into the hot tub instead. This time, no one was there.

"This is way better than the last time," she said.

"I don't want anyone else in here."

"It seems a little slow today."

"Not at the pool," he said. "Cool water would have been nice after mini golf."

"What, and miss reliving our last hot tub escapade but *without* me sitting on your lap? What a shame."

"Shame isn't the right word."

"What—you *enjoyed* me sitting on your lap?"

"There was one part of me that very much enjoyed that." His voice was low—the type of near mutter he'd only used with her.

"One part does not equal the whole man."

"Fine. Then, *all* of me was happy with you on my lap. I had just wished we were alone for that."

"I mean, we're *mostly* alone now. We could try again."

He stared over at her, his eyes dark. Her throat went dry, and she wondered if he would turn her down. Maybe it would have been better if he had.

All of the fears she clung to lost their grip on her as he looked at her with his brown eyes.

"Come over here."

Amelia didn't waste any time. She crossed the small hot tub, but instead of turning around to sit in his lap, she stayed facing him.

"Can we agree to add in some creative differences this time?"

His hands landed on her hips. "We definitely can."

This wasn't for show. None of her family was around, and she wouldn't *want* them to be. This was for her. She had to give into her desires, or else they would eat her alive.

She had been attracted to Daniel for so long and near him so much this week that she simply *wanted* him. For now, she wasn't concerned by the strings or the aftermath.

Daniel's hand cupped her face. "Do you know what else I'd like to relive?"

"I hope it's last night's kiss."

"You read my mind." He inched closer, and her heart leaped in her chest as he tilted his head toward her. They kissed, slowly and tentatively at first. But then his grip tightened as he moved his lips against hers, kissing her the way he had the night before.

She could lose herself in this. The background faded away as his lips slid over hers. She forgot where she was—who she was. She could only think of him.

Then her knee barely scraped the concrete of the hot tub.

"Let's go back to the room," she said, pulling away. "I think I want some privacy for the rest of this." Her eyes lingered on his lips. But now, all she could think about was getting *more* from him.

Nothing had ever felt like this, and she wasn't sure anything else could. She got out of the hot tub and grabbed their towels. She left his with him and darted up to the condo, anticipation traveling up her spine.

No one was home, which she thanked her lucky stars for. Daniel wasted no time in following her, and he kissed her the moment the door to their room shut.

He walked her backward and she didn't know where they were going until she felt tile under her feet.

"We should shower," he said.

"Like we stop this to shower or . . ."

"I say we multitask."

"I *love* multitasking," she breathed out.

She practically ripped off her bathing suit as the shower turned on. There was a moment when air rushed over her body, and she wondered if he liked what he saw. But then a low groan erupted from his throat, and he pulled her under the spray of the showerhead. It took her a moment to realize he was naked too.

Amelia was awash with sensation. She could feel the water on her skin, his lips on hers, and the press of his cock against her stomach. She reached down to grip it, feeling it fill her hand. He broke the kiss, nearly panting.

"God, Amelia. You don't know what you do to me." His voice was rough.

"Maybe I want to."

"I thought about this. About you. Ever since I saw you in that swimsuit, I couldn't stop thinking about what I could do to you."

Her heart hammered. "Show me now."

Daniel set her against the shower wall, the cool tile an oasis to her overheated skin. She could feel him press against her stomach again, and her core clenched. She needed that in her.

"D-do you—" She struggled to find her voice. "—happen to have condoms somewhere?"

He paused. "I don't. I didn't think this would ever . . . Should we stop?"

"There are other things we can do," she said. "With hands and mouths."

"That sounds perfect. And I'm clear of anything, just so you know. I got tested a while ago."

"Me too. The moment we're not in the shower, we can fix our condom problem. But for now—" She pushed him away from her and sank to her knees. "I would like to do this. Is that okay?"

"Yes," he hissed out.

When her mouth came around him, she could hear his shaky breath. She took him as far as he could go into the back of her throat, slowly, wrapping her hand around the rest of him. At his muttered curses, she sped up, pulling her cheeks in.

Daniel was heavy in her mouth. She lost herself in giving him pleasure, her body humming at each of his groans. She loved making other people feel good, especially when they were as considerate as he'd been for this whole trip.

Water poured on her, but she didn't care. Her entire focus was on making him feel as good as possible. His hips began moving, jerking forward. His breathing picked up speed.

She risked a glance up at him. Gone was the man who she knew. Instead, she saw someone lost in pleasure, with water dripping off his curly hair. His eyes were shut, and he leaned against the shower wall to the side of him.

She'd done that. She'd made him feel like this.

"Yes, just like that," he muttered. "Good. You're doing so good."

Her body purred in response.

And she was going to keep doing it until he came, feeling empowered by his reactions.

She was patient, working him up to the brink of orgasm, listening to each sound he made.

"Fuck," he said, pulling out of her. His come shot out of him, landing on her chest and face.

She blinked, not expecting him to pull out.

His chest heaved as she stood and stepped close to him. "I hope that was—"

His mouth closed over hers, and she let out a squeak of surprise. Daniel's hands gripped her hips, pushing her back against the wall. Her mind couldn't comprehend that he was touching her. He'd gotten what he wanted—shouldn't he be done?

"We can finish up," she said, pulling away.

"Do you really think I'm done with you?"

"Um, yes?"

"Amelia." He said her name low. "I'm just getting started."

This wasn't how things went—at least in her experience—but she refused to complain. His mouth moved to her neck and his hands cupped her breasts, her body coming alive as his palms brushed her hardened nipples.

She didn't notice until now, but she'd been desperate for contact. A broken gasp escaped her as he gently pinched one of her nipples.

"Do you like that?" he asked.

"Yes," she said. "I really do."

She closed her eyes as his hand moved again. She didn't notice when his mouth left her neck. The only thing she felt was his mouth latch around her other nipple.

Her pussy throbbed, feeling left out of all the attention.

"D-Daniel, *please*," she managed to say. "I need . . ."

"What do you need?" His breath ghosted on her nipple, a new kind of torture.

"I need you to touch me. Please, just touch me."

His hand and mouth left her breasts and she bemoaned the lack of sensation.

"Here?" he asked before kissing her rib cage.

"Lower."

"Here?" He was at her stomach.

"N-no. Come on, *please* just—"

He coaxed her legs open, and she propped one foot on the edge of the tub.

"Here?" She felt his breath on her center.

"Yes."

His tongue met her clit and she saw stars. There was no more talking for her, only feeling. His tongue provided a perfectly crushing pressure. He circled the bud of nerves, sucked at it, and sent her into space with his mouth.

Was this how he had felt when she had been on her knees? Because this was *life-changing*.

"I'm going to use my hands," he said, pulling inches away. "Is that okay?"

"Sure," she said. Amelia would miss his mouth, but she didn't mind him switching it up if he was tired. Some men didn't like going down on women. Andrew sure hadn't.

But Daniel's mouth closed back down on her most sensitive part, and his hand moved up. She quickly realized that she had misunderstood what he meant by using his hands. One finger teased at her entrance, slowly pushing its way in.

"Oh my God," she moaned. His finger curved, hitting her G-spot. Just how coordinated was this man? And how the *hell* did Lucinda let him go?

A second finger joined in, pushing her closer to her own release. His tongue was talented, but his fingers even more so.

"D-Daniel," she stuttered, "I'm gonna—"

"Come on me, Amelia. I want to feel it."

And that shot her over the edge. He had only barely gotten his mouth back on her when her orgasm hit. Every nerve ending pulsed in white-hot pleasure. She felt it shoot from her toes to her fingertips. This was a release like none other, and as it coursed through her, she wondered if anything could be better than this.

When she came down from her high, the shower water was cold. Daniel slowly got up, eyes dark as they settled on her.

"We need condoms," he said. "Because when you do that again, I want it to be my cock you come on."

She must have passed out because she had to be dreaming.

If she was, however, then it was the greatest dream she could ever have.

CHAPTER EIGHTEEN

DANIEL

They didn't have much energy after their shower. Or at least, Amelia didn't seem to.

And while his orgasm had been mind-altering, seeing *hers* had been even better. He planned to go to the supermarket down the road to get the condoms they desperately needed, but then she laid her head on his shoulder and fell asleep, and he knew there was no moving.

He drifted off, her weight comfortable on him. When he woke up, they'd barely moved, but his hands had drifted under her shirt, and he could feel himself harden at the reminder of what they'd done in the shower.

He definitely should have gotten the condoms the night before.

This was the last full day of the vacation and he didn't know if this new development would carry over to their normal lives in the way their fake relationship would. But he wanted it to. He needed more than just one full day with her.

Amelia slowly opened her eyes. She blinked a few times, as if trying to gauge where she was, and then she looked at him. A small smile made its way onto her face.

"Hi," she said sleepily.

Daniel couldn't help but return the smile. "Hey."

"So, last night wasn't a dream, right?"

"Not unless we both had it."

She smiled again and kissed him, which did nothing but further his desire for her. He pressed himself against her almost instinctively.

She reached down, giving him just the slightest bit of friction on his aching—

"Amelia! Daniel! Do you want to go to breakfast?"

"Damn it," she muttered. "I feel like a teenager getting caught with a boy in her room. Do you want breakfast?"

He was hungry, but not for food.

"Sure," he said. "We have errands to run after anyway."

"We'll go!" Amelia called back. "And if you mean condoms," she added lowly, "I will *not* be buying those with my parents present."

"Understandable."

"And it's not even for the reason you think." Amelia got up and picked out her outfit. "When my mom found out, she took me to the drugstore to show me every kind of condom I could ever need.

The only problem? The guy I was *with* walked in." She shuddered. "Worst day of my life."

"As mortifying as that is, at least you were educated."

"Oh yeah. Down to the *sizing*. He walked in on me saying that I needed a smaller size."

"No. He didn't."

"He did. I had to have a long talk with him about how it didn't matter to me and how I liked him either way. He still ghosted me though."

"Then he missed out."

She turned to him, smiling with narrowed eyes. "You're just saying that because of the blow job."

"No. It's much more than—"

"We're ready when you are!" Mandy called.

"You should get dressed," Amelia said. "We can't keep them waiting for long."

He did as he was told, getting dressed in record time. Amelia disappeared for only a second, muttering that she needed to do one other thing before she left. She grabbed her bag and darted from the room.

For a moment, he wondered if she was hiding something from him.

Or someone.

It would make sense—why else would she be up on her sexual health if she wasn't sleeping with other people? She'd only said she didn't want a relationship, but she could easily have other partners.

She's not Lucinda, he reminded himself. And besides, this might all be casual for Amelia too. They hadn't had a chance to talk about what any of this was.

They *did* need to talk about it at some point.

But this wasn't the moment for that discussion. For now, he finished getting ready and then met everyone by the door. She had been chugging a glass of water when he got out.

She gave him a thumbs-up that he wasn't sure what to do with, but he attributed it to their change in relationship. He gave her space as they walked to the car.

"So," she began, looking out the window, "we went a whole night before it got awkward. That's a record for me."

"It's not awkward."

"Your face says otherwise," she said. "When you came out of the room, you seemed . . . different."

"It's just something we have to talk about later. That's all."

"You know those are the worst words I could hear, right?" She laughed, but it didn't sound like she was amused. "I mean, we have to talk about something *later*? And it has you upset?" Her fingers tapped on her knee. "That's not worrying me at all."

"It's nothing bad."

"Then why can't we talk about it now?"

"It's . . . I don't know how to ask."

"Anything is better than nothing."

"Okay, then. Is there anyone else?"

There was only silence. His heart kicked up speed.

"Wh-what? Anyone else with what?"

"You. I mean in general."

"Like *with* as in sexually?"

"Yes."

"Why are you asking?"

"Because when you ran out, I got the idea that you're hiding something, and the last time someone was hiding something was when Lucinda was with my dad."

The car was silent, and he wondered if it was proof of an omission.

"Oh, *shit*. First of all, no. There is no one else and there will be no one else. I'm not . . . I would never . . ." She shuddered.

He risked a glance at her. "Really?"

"Yes, really. I don't have some guy back home that I sleep with, nor do I here. And I wouldn't go back to them even if I did. Our relationship might be fake, but I'm still dedicated to it."

"Thank God," he replied. "I'm sorry I even brought it up. I must have been in the wrong state of mind this morning."

"It's okay," she said. "It's something we should clear up anyway."

Her voice was small, and she looked back out the window. Daniel wondered what was running through her head, but they pulled into the breakfast restaurant right after, and Mandy was waiting on them.

"Last day at the beach!" she said, blissfully unaware of any of the lingering awkwardness between them. "I almost don't want this to end."

"We'll come back next year," Randy said. "Now, let's get in there. I'm dying for some waffles."

Daniel knew he needed to get back to being Amelia's perfect boyfriend, but as they walked in, he wondered if he'd made a mistake in questioning her at all. Most people would have been upset to be accused of keeping secrets.

But she seemed okay. She sat next to him, giving him a small smile.

There was no one else, and that helped him far more than he could express.

"So what do you do for fun, Daniel?" John asked, pulling him out of his thoughts.

"Fun? Unfortunately, my work schedule doesn't allow for much of that."

"That's not good for you. Do you like working out? I live in Atlanta too. Maybe we can hang out."

"That could be nice," he replied, but he saw Amelia's confused expression in the corner of his eye.

Maybe it would have been better to turn John down, but he liked this family. John seemed like the kind of person he could get along with.

It wouldn't last. Once his and Amelia's fake relationship was over, so would his fledgling friendship with her brother.

He could enjoy it while it lasted, though.

"What is this?" Amelia said. "You're connecting with my boyfriend?"

"I like this one," John said. "We all do."

He gave Amelia a pointed look, but her eyes darted away.

Daniel glanced over at her, feeling like there was a whole conversation he was missing out on.

"And you're always welcome out at our house in the middle of nowhere," Randy added. "Though it may not be your thing."

"It sounds nice." He only wished he could see it.

They were interrupted by a waitress coming to take their order, and it hit Daniel just how much he could see living this life forever. With Amelia and her family.

After breakfast, they drove back to the condo, Daniel's mind still on what could have been.

"S-so, you and John."

"I don't have to talk to him again."

"No," she said. "It's not that. He just usually doesn't go out of his way to connect with others. It's a compliment, really."

"I don't want to make it harder for when this ends," he said. "So I won't worry about it."

"Yeah, about that . . . How long did you want to do this for when we get back?"

That was a complicated answer. "I didn't have a date in mind."

"Right, and with the news, I bet it'll last a while."

"Yes, but we don't have to pretend for very long if you don't want to. I'm sure news like that will linger for months."

"I said I would pretend to be your girlfriend until it died down. If it's months, then . . . I'm fine with that too."

"Because you want to or because you feel like you have to?"

Her cheeks turned pink. "I want to. And if in that time period, you did want to take John up on his offer, then do it. I don't mind. Maybe I could start running regularly too."

"I think I'd like that."

"You know what else I'd like?" she asked. "To enjoy the waves on our last day here. Want to go for a swim?"

"Don't we have errands to run? We could go to Target."

Amelia's nose scrunched, and he remembered how badly their previous Target trip had gone. "Can we just skip it for now? I think I want to be in the water. We go back tomorrow anyway, and I have plenty of what we need back in Atlanta."

"That works for me."

They arrived at the condo and immediately went down to the beach. The salty air simmered with the memories of the night before, but she seemed content to enjoy the water, and this was their last chance to.

By the end of the day, Daniel had forgotten about all of his problems.

But then, when he was toweling off, he finally checked his phone.

Lucinda: We're telling everyone tomorrow.

His heart sank. At least his father had given him a week.

Terri: You free? I need an update on your wild adventure.

"Mind if I call my sister?" he asked. "We need to catch up."

"Of course not," she replied. "I'll see you back in the room."

Daniel watched her go before calling Terri.

"Hey," he said. "Sorry, I was away from my phone for a bit."

"Don't be," she replied. "It's nice that you're away from it for once. How is it going?"

"Lucinda and Dad are telling everyone tomorrow."

"Oh, perfect," Terri said dryly. "I'm guessing he told you?"

"She did," he said. "She's been acting weird since finding out about Amelia."

"I'm sure she has. Leave it to her to cheat on you, then want you to stay single forever. Good riddance." Terri blew a raspberry.

"How much wine have you had?"

"None, but the actions of a kid carry over after a while." She sighed. "And he's in the other room, so I can't say what I'm really thinking."

"I get it," he replied. "Amelia overheard me snap at Lucinda and I had to tell her who she left me for. It was awkward, to say the least, but she'd find out eventually. Luckily for me, she's not the biggest fan of Lucinda, either."

"Really? And how are things going with the beautiful Amelia?"

"Fine."

"Any feelings turn real?"

"Maybe."

"And has anything happened?"

"Why do you want to know?"

"Chrissy and I have a bet. Mine is that you'll break before the vacation is up. I'll win twenty dollars."

"Then consider yourself twenty dollars richer."

"Yes! Now, are you officially together, or is this one of those things where you don't talk about it, and it inevitably blows up in your face?"

"We're not official, but we did agree to be committed to the fake relationship."

"Wow, communication, huh? Is she still not wanting to date anyone?"

"I think so."

"So, how long does this little ruse go on for?"

"No clue. We agreed to end it whenever. Could be months."

Terri laughed. "Months? Sounds like a real relationship."

"Maybe one day."

"Start getting her favorite foods. I'll plan on making her a table at Thanksgiving, and you two can tell this epic story to us over dinner."

"I don't know that it's going to end up like that."

"We'll see. Just tell me if she likes green bean casserole or sweet potatoes, okay?"

"And if you're wrong?"

"I'll make deviled eggs just for you. Now, get back to your vacation. I need to tell Chrissy all of this."

They said their goodbyes, and Daniel took a minute to think on his sister's words. He could still see it all happening.

But he could only hope it would actually come to fruition.

Amelia was asleep by the time he got back. She was on top of the covers, looking as if she'd fallen asleep on accident.

He got her under the covers before showering and pulling out his book to read. He didn't get very far into it before the exhaustion from the day hit him, and he followed her into sleep.

***

A resounding knock on the door alerted them both.

"Hey, lovebirds," Mandy called through the door. "We have to check out soon."

"Okay!" Amelia called back. "Be out soon!"

As consciousness returned to him, a somber reminder flashed in his head.

Today is the day.

"We have so much to do," she groaned. "I didn't pack at all last night."

They really hadn't.

"I'll start," he said, eager to get his mind off of what was coming. He got up, immediately putting everything in his suitcase. Amelia helped, and they were ready within an hour.

"Are you guys all done?" Mandy asked as they stood outside Amelia's car.

"Yep," Amelia answered. "We should head back and start preparing for work on Monday."

"I get it, but we should all go out to lunch now that I'm feeling better."

"There's always the pizza place by our office."

After hugging Amelia tightly, Mandy threw her arms around him too.

"Now, don't be a stranger," she said, pulling away. "We really liked spending this week with you, even if you only had eyes for Amelia."

Daniel felt his face heat up, and he awkwardly laughed, trying to play it off.

"It's fine," Mandy said. "That means you like her, and that's all I wanted."

"I really do," he admitted.

"I guess I'll see you soon. Both of you, hopefully."

"Nice to have met you, son," Randy said, stepping forward to give Daniel's hand a shake. "You're a good one."

"You too," Daniel replied with a smile.

"It's so weird not to be riding back with you," Amelia added.

"It is, but I know coming back to our house makes the trip longer," Mandy said. "Plus, you have an amazing driver with you."

"Hah, that's right. I'm so glad not to have to drive back alone," Amelia said. Daniel smiled at her before John pulled him aside to exchange numbers.

"I'm serious about you two working out. Both in the gym and in general. You suit each other."

An uncomfortable feeling settled in his chest. "Thanks, John."

"Just . . . be patient, okay? I think her ex did more than she says."

"I know the feeling," he replied truthfully. He wondered if he would have ever admitted what Lucinda did if it weren't for her and his father telling the world.

"Ready to go?" Amelia asked, walking over to him.

"I think so." To John, Daniel said, "Thanks for giving me your number."

"No problem. See you guys soon."

They waved goodbye before getting into the car. Daniel sat in the driver's seat automatically, hoping his father would hold off just until they got back to Atlanta.

"I didn't expect them to like you so much."

"Really?"

"I don't mean that in a bad way," she rushed to say. Her face was red. "I just meant that before you came, you were a different person, at least to me. I expected you to be all business."

"I think I expected to just fake my way through this trip and never be myself."

"I like the real side of you," she admitted quietly. "It's nice."

He had to fight the urge to look over at her.

And that was when his phone jingled. His heart picked up speed. Could it be the announcement?

Another notification came in. And then another one.

"You know," he said, his voice tight, "maybe we should top off the tank before we get too into driving."

"That's a good idea. Go for it."

When they pulled into the gas station, Amelia went inside to use the bathroom and grab a coffee while Daniel pulled out his phone.

Michael Anderson had announced he was getting married to Lucinda Jackson—and he'd tagged Daniel in the post.

People he went to college with who knew Lucinda were messaging him, asking questions.

Is this really your father?

Didn't you marry her?

She's with WHO?

"Fuck," Daniel muttered as he read through them all. His stomach churned.

The car door flew open. "Did he tag you in a post?"

"How did you know?"

"Mom is your Facebook friend. She saw it."

"Your *mom* saw it?"

"She doesn't know Lucinda is your ex."

Daniel groaned.

"That *asshole*," she snarled, shaking her head. "What can I do?"

"I don't know. I have people messaging me and I don't know what to say to them."

"Do you have to say anything?"

"I . . . I don't know. I'm so overwhelmed, and the messages keep coming."

Amelia took the phone out of his hands, and he blinked over at her, confused.

"Those people can wait," she said. "I think you need a minute to breathe."

"But—"

"You know what your dad said, and you know what he posted. You don't owe anyone an explanation."

It felt wrong to just put his phone away. So many people were probably waiting to hear his side of the story. They had to want to know what was going on.

But he didn't want to explain it yet. While he was over his ex, he didn't want to share the sordid story with people he hadn't talked to in years. He didn't want to stare at the post of Lucinda and his father, of all people, remembering the night he'd found out what she'd done.

"You're right," he said softly. "I need a break."

"I'll hold onto this. Are you okay to drive?"

"Yeah, I am. If I'm driving, I can't look at social media."

He drove on autopilot, listening to the near silence of the car.

But then, even that was shattered by his ringtone. He'd totally forgotten that he hooked up Bluetooth while he was driving. They both glanced at the screen in the car, and Daniel cursed when he saw it was his father.

"Don't answer it," she urged.

"He'll just keep calling," he said through gritted teeth. Before he could think twice, he pressed the answer button on the steering wheel. "What?" Daniel said, too annoyed to answer with anything else.

"You saw my post, right?" his father asked. Out of the corner of his eye, he saw Amelia's jaw drop.

"I did."

"What do you think? Does it express my love well enough?"

Daniel should have been shocked by that question, and yet he wasn't. He was more embarrassed that Amelia had to hear any of this. He didn't even want to risk any more glances over at her.

"It's fine, Dad," Daniel said, his voice tight.

"Well, you should like it, son. And let me know if you're coming to the wedding. Lucinda wants you there."

He didn't know what to say to that. It was all he could do to focus on driving. He'd much rather be screaming.

"Actually, he's busy," Amelia said, and Daniel was shocked to hear her speak up. "Very busy, actually."

"Daniel, who is that?"

"I'm his girlfriend, Amelia. And Daniel here is going to be busy with me during your wedding."

"It's his father's—"

"Nope, I don't care who you are. You're not forcing my boyfriend to do anything he doesn't want to. So stop asking," she said. "In fact, I think it's weird for my boyfriend to go to his ex-wife's wedding, so we're not going to do that. Let your son have some time to deal with you stealing his wife. Okay? Bye now."

Amelia hung up the call.

"What was that?" Daniel asked incredulously.

"That was me making a decision. He's a self-righteous ass."

"He's going to call back."

"Oh, I know. Your phone is on silent now."

"But he's going to get mad."

"Like you're not also mad?"

"I am."

"So why even give him the time of day?"

He didn't have an answer. For a long time, he'd dealt with his father with a distant acceptance. Sure, he would only talk about himself, but Daniel could deal with it when he called. After all, he knew Terri wanted the updates despite her being disowned.

Then his father wound up with Lucinda, and things got worse.

"I don't know. Maybe I shouldn't."

"You don't owe him anything, even if he is your dad."

Randy had said something similar.

"You're right," Daniel said. "I'm not answering for the rest of the day."

"I think that's the right call. Besides, I doubt anything good will come of it."

He hoped she was right.

"Are you going to be okay?"

"Probably," he replied. "Maybe."

"I know this is a weird situation, but is there anything I can do to help?"

Daniel wasn't sure. All he knew was that he was overwhelmed and tired of dealing with it. It didn't help that after a week of having Amelia close to him nearly all the time, he would be back in his empty apartment alone.

"Daniel?" she asked. "You still in there?"

"Kind of. I think I might need a break from driving."

"Pull off. I'll take it from here."

Once they'd switched, he looked out the window distantly. In his mind, he was replaying the Facebook announcement over and over. He could just hear his father saying it. He could feel Lucinda's smile as he hit post, as if she had won.

But the feeling of her winning didn't bother him. Going back to the place that they had shared did.

"We're getting close to the city," she said. "Do you want me to drop you off?"

"That would be great."

It didn't take them long to get to his place. He told Amelia to pull into his second parking spot, but it was taken.

He stared at the blue sports car, horror washing over him.

"Huh," she said, ignorant of his worry. "A neighbor must be having a guest over."

"That's not a guest. That's Lucinda."

"What? What would she be doing here?"

"She shows up from time to time."

"Oh, come on." Amelia threw the car in reverse and found the guest parking.

"What are you doing?" he asked as she cut the engine.

"Going in with you. I'm not letting you do this alone."

"You don't have to."

"I want to," she said. "Unless you *don't* want me to."

"I do. Please. I can't keep dealing with this alone."

"Then you won't."

His apartment was on the second floor, and Amelia followed him up the stairs quietly.

Daniel took out his key and turned the lock. His body was tight with anxiety.

Amelia put a warm hand on his shoulder. "We've got this."

He opened the door, only to be hit with the scent of Lucinda's perfume. It immediately took him back to their marriage, as it always did. The nights she would make him pose for the perfect Instagram selfie, or the nights where they would fight when he was far too tired for sex. It sent chills up his spine.

"Yuck, someone needs to air out the place." Amelia fanned the air around her, face set in a scowl. He'd only seen her this protective at work when an employee came to her asking for help. He didn't know how he'd somehow become a person she cared enough about to protect, but it calmed him in the face of his ex-wife.

Lucinda rounded the corner, coming into the foyer. She was dressed in one of her white robes, which was nothing more than a tiny silk dress. She looked like she had never left.

"Oh, Daniel. You're *finally* back," she announced.

"He's not back for you," Amelia said dryly. "That's for sure."

Lucinda blinked as if finally realizing he wasn't alone.

"Who are you?" Lucinda's voice soured.

"I'm his girlfriend," Amelia replied, and he felt his heart stutter at her words. "What are you doing here?"

"I live here."

"No, you don't," he replied.

Lucinda pouted, her lower lip poking out in a pitiful way. "But I picked this place out."

"When we were married," he snapped.

"Come on, you can't be mad at me for missing you."

"Yes, I can. Especially when you're with my father now. Did you come here to rub it in again, or are you getting bored?"

"Shouldn't you care more?"

"I do care, but not about you. I care that you've embarrassed me, and I care that you're invading my privacy, but I don't care about you. That stopped the moment you cheated on me."

"In a gross way too," Amelia said. "I hope you know anyone with sense thinks you're a gold digger. Besides"—Amelia turned to Daniel—"is she even on the lease?"

"Not anymore."

Amelia turned back to Lucinda, who was glaring at her. "So, you're trespassing."

"I've seen you before," Lucinda said after a moment. "Where?"

Amelia's voice came out flat. "I work with him. I'm the head of HR, and the reason you're not allowed in the building."

Daniel had never mentioned Amelia, but in the rare times Lucinda would come to the office to show off their relationship, she would see his coworker and mutter something about having to stake a claim to ward off the pretty women in the office.

Lucinda's blue eyes dawned with recognition. "*You're* his new girlfriend?" she asked. "*You?*"

"Yep."

"So I had a right to be worried. You *did* have feelings for someone else."

"Daniel and I only got together *after* you left," Amelia cut in. "Unlike you, I understood that he had loyalty to his wife, up until you cheated and divorced him, that is."

Lucinda looked Amelia up and down, and Daniel knew what she was about to do.

"Don't," he muttered.

"If you're going after *my* man, at least you could tame that frizz. Or lose a few pounds. Whichever is easier."

Daniel closed his eyes, knowing how much an insult like that could sting.

But Amelia laughed. "Is that all you could come up with? At least be a little more creative with it. Here, I'll go first. You have the smell of a dog who was chased down by a skunk after not having a bath for six months. You have the personality of dry bread pretending to be toast. *And* you lost Daniel. A long time ago. So go back to pretending that your new man is perfect for you and find someone else to prey on. He's taken."

"Oh, you think you're funny, don't you? I had him first, and I can wear him down."

"You're not going to," he said. "You're just an annoyance. I don't even know how you got in, considering I changed the locks."

"The doorman is *very* interested in our relationship. He wants us together."

"It must have really bothered you that Daniel was with me for a week out of town," Amelia said. She slowly turned to him. "Do you want to stay with me? It'll be better than here."

His heart picked up speed. He wanted that more than anything, but he had no idea if she meant it or not. "Yes," he said. "That would be great."

"What?" Lucinda squawked. "But—"

"We're going to be very busy packing," Amelia said. "I'd been meaning to ask him to stay over tonight. Thanks, Lucinda."

"You little—"

"Out!" Daniel snapped. "Or do I need to let your new fiancé know where you are?"

Lucinda's eyes went wild for a moment, and he briefly wondered if she was going to lunge at them.

But then she ran.

"Man," Amelia said, "she is a piece of work."

"Dry bread pretending to be toast?"

"When my brain works with me, I can come up with devastating things to say to people I don't like. Plus, I'd been working on those. I'm not her biggest fan."

"Me either," he replied. "Thank you for helping me get her out of here."

"She'll be back," she warned. "Which is why my offer to stay with me was real. You're welcome at my place. Until you get bored of me, of course."

"I don't think I will." He felt his lips break into a smile. "I was hoping it was a real offer. Or else I'd be a little disappointed."

"I'd hate to disappoint, but shouldn't you be tired of me by now? We've spent a week always with each other."

"I'm not tired of you. Are you tired of me?"

"No."

"Good. Hopefully, from here, there will be less drama. Until Lucinda calls, I guess." As he said it, his phone lit up with a call. "Isn't this on silent?"

"I put it on quiet mode, but someone insistent can get past it." They both looked at this screen; it showed Lucinda's name. "She literally just left, and now she's calling you too?" He could hear the annoyance in her voice.

"She always does this whenever she wants attention."

"Are you going to answer?"

"No, but she's going to keep calling."

"Why not block her?"

Daniel sighed. "If I block her, then my father will start asking questions."

"Then, block him too."

"He's my father."

"And what do you owe him? Other than him being your mom's sperm donor?"

She wasn't wrong, but he didn't know if he could go through with it. "My family sometimes wants updates. Especially my sister. He disowned her after she came out."

"Would she be mad if you stopped talking to him?"

"No, but I know I'm her last connection to him, and blocking him feels like it's bigger than just me."

"You don't have to keep making yourself miserable, though, even if she wants updates. Besides, I've rocked the boat today, and both of them are going to be mad."

"Maybe I'll ask her about it next time we talk," he said. "But for now, I can do this." He turned off his phone.

"That's a good call. Now, let's get packed up and out of here. I don't like the way it smells."

After he packed, they wasted no time getting to Amelia's place.

She lived in an older apartment building on the second floor. When he walked in, he could see how the place fit her personality. She had teal decorations and photos of her with her family and friends lining the walls. It was lived-in, not just for show. She gave him a quick tour, even clearing off the pillows on one side of her bed for him.

"Thank you for letting me stay," he said.

"You're welcome. But in the interest of being a good host, I have to go get some food. I was thinking of going to Trader Joe's. Want to join?"

Daniel hadn't been shopping with anyone in years. It hadn't been Lucinda's idea of a fun time. "Sure," he said. "I need to get a few things anyway."

***

Shopping with Amelia, he quickly learned, was not a focused task. She first got distracted by the flyer in the front of the store. Then she saw a kid with a miniature shopping cart and told their mom how sweet it was. Then she found the flowers.

"When I was a kid, I always used to say I wanted my wedding bouquet to be pink and orange," she explained, gently reaching out to touch the petals. "But we came here for food. Sorry, I keep getting distracted."

"It's fine," he replied. "We can look at the flowers if you want to."

She bit her lip. "Are you sure?"

"Yeah. These are the things I wouldn't ever look at before. I think it's time for me to start."

"Okay," she said. "Then what's your favorite?"

He pointed out a blue and white arrangement a few feet away. They walked through the corner of the store, looking at each one.

"I've got to say—" She went back to the pink and orange one. "—this is my favorite."

"Then we'll get it."

"Wh-what? We don't have to—"

"If it's your favorite, then I'll get it for you. What kind of boyfriend would I be if I didn't get you flowers?" He picked them up and offered them to her.

"Wow," she said, sounding breathless. "You go all out, huh?"

"I'm working myself up to level three. Isn't that the highest?"

"That's the one where you know all the weird things about me," she said, gingerly taking the bouquet from him, "so yes."

"How am I doing?"

Her cheeks were a delicate shade of pink. "Pretty good."

Daniel was tempted to bring her into a kiss. It didn't matter that no one was watching or that this was fake. He simply wanted to feel her lips against his again.

"Oh my God," a voice said. "Daniel, is that you?"

He blinked, turning to his right.

"Dana," Daniel said. "Hi."

"I can't believe I ran into you," she said. "You look so . . . *relaxed*." Her eyes went to his hair, which was unstyled, and then to the woman beside him. "Amelia? You're here too?"

"Oh, hi," Amelia said, putting the flowers in the cart. "What a small world."

"Did we all run into each other here?" Dana asked. "What are the odds?"

"No, Amelia and I came here together."

Dana blinked. "T-together?"

He risked a glance over at Amelia, silently asking if this was okay. They may have agreed to do this relationship at work, but he needed to make sure she hadn't changed her mind.

She gave him the tiniest of nods.

"Yes," he said. "Together."

"Shopping together," Dana said. "And you were both gone the same week. Wait, does that mean—"

"We're dating?" Amelia asked for her. "Yes."

Dana looked between them, then shook her head. "I didn't even know you were ready to date again, Daniel."

He frowned, the statement throwing him off. "I don't usually discuss my dating life with my employees."

"But Amelia . . ."

"Isn't my employee," he finished.

"Oh," she said with a frown of her own.

"We won't take up much of your time," Amelia said, grabbing his arm. "We need to get back to my apartment."

She dragged him away before he could say anything else. He didn't give much resistance. He didn't want to talk to Dana for too long anyway.

"Was that weird to you?" he asked.

"Definitely, but it will get the rumor mill turning." She smiled up at him. "Good job."

He nodded, looking over his shoulder at Dana. Her eyes were still on them.

"Maybe we should hold hands," he said. "To make it more realistic."

"You're a level two-boyfriend, Daniel," she said, sliding her hand into his. "Almost level three. You don't have to ask."

She pulled him deeper into the store, continuing to get groceries. He grabbed the few lunch and breakfast items he wanted, following along as she meandered through the store, looking at everything that caught her eye.

In the end, they had a full cart and a completed grocery list.

"I can't wait to try that coffee I found," she said as they walked to the car. "Maybe it'll energize me enough to be excited for work."

"With how nice that vacation was, I doubt either of us will have fun at work."

"Other people will. I imagine Dana has told half the staff by now."

"They were probably already talking too," he said.

"At least you have this to cover up Lucinda." She bumped her shoulder with his. "That should help."

He nodded, helping her get the bags into the car. Once they got back to her apartment, they put it all up and made a quick dinner.

"You know, this is kind of nice," she said as they cleaned up after eating. "Maybe not vacation-level nice, but still great."

"This is still a vacation to me," he said. "Being away from that apartment is more relaxing than you know."

She set the last dish in the sink and dried off her hands. "More relaxing than a hot tub?"

His skin heated at the memory. "If you're talking about the one at the condo, then I wouldn't call that hot tub relaxing."

"Then what would you call it?"

He could still feel the press of her ass in his lap and the way her lips felt against his. "I don't have a good word, but I will always remember it. Every second of it."

"Really?" Her voice lowered. "And what about the shower?"

"Even better."

"Do you want to know what's *really* great about being home?" She smiled. "I have condoms here, if that's what you want, of course. It's been a long day."

"I can't think of a better way to end it."

Amelia was the woman who'd supported him all day—acting like a partner he never knew he needed. The night in the shower was always in the back of his mind, and this new emotional connection made him want her even more.

She stepped close to him, and he could see the depths of her brown eyes only for a second before she kissed him.

His heart picked up speed as her lips slid against his. His hand moved up to cup her cheek, and he couldn't help but wish this was real and this could be his life from now on.

But then her body pressed against his, and all thoughts flew out the window. Her tongue met his and their kiss became frantic.

He was calculating how to get to the bedroom when she pushed them onto the couch. He fell, her weight on top of him. His hands couldn't decide what part of her to touch first, whether it be her hips, her ass, or her back, and all thoughts of even making it to the bedroom dissolved.

His cock was aching at the thought of having her this close. She ground down, giving him a taste of delectable friction. He could feel his own breath stutter as she moved against him.

"We need less layers," he managed to say.

"You're so right," she replied. She sat up, pulling off her top. She then turned those brown eyes to him and got up. He was about to pull her close again, but she was working at his pants, pulling them off. "Happy now?"

"Not until all of yours are off." He sat up too, removing her leggings in turn, then ripped his own shirt up over his head. Amelia left for a brief moment to grab a condom. Once he had it on, she took her rightful place on top of him.

His cock rubbed against her, and he caught her sharp intake of breath. He arched his hips up, noticing how her eyes closed.

"Good?" he asked.

Amelia nodded, her breath coming out fast.

He continued his work, watching her exquisite reactions as he made sure she felt good. Making her come was one of his new favorite things to do. And his own arousal only grew as he watched her pleasure.

Her hips met his, and she chased after what she needed. Her grip on his shoulders tightened and he could see the moment she broke. Her mouth fell open, body twitching as her orgasm sent her over the edge.

After she had a moment to collect herself, she finally looked at him. "That was amazing," she said.

"Should I call you my good girl now?"

Her cheeks were red. "You remembered that?"

"I was mostly joking," he replied. "Both then and now."

"What if I said I liked it?"

"Then I'll remember that for next time." And there *definitely* would be a next time.

"But you can't call me that now." She gave him a devious smile. "Because I think I'm done being good. Now it's your turn."

She angled herself so his cock caught her entrance. As she slowly took him, inch by inch, he saw stars.

God, she felt unreal. So tight and hot and responsive. It was mental work not to come then and there. Her tight grip on his shoulders hadn't relented.

"Are you okay?" he asked.

"More than okay. This is possibly the best I've ever been. But now I need you to move."

Daniel's hands gripped her hips, and he thrust up.

"Oh fuck," she said.

He moved her legs to get impossibly deeper, and his control finally snapped.

He went on like that for as long as he could, feeling her push back into him every time he slowed, but he couldn't take much more.

But then she gasped, moving her hips in time with his. He could see her about to crumble, her facial expression a mirror of just moments ago when she'd come.

He could feel her clench around him as she continued to breathe heavily. Her orgasm sent him into his, and he could feel shock waves shoot through his entire body.

When he could breathe again, he noticed her barely catching her own breath.

"You're incredible," he hummed as he came down from his high.

She looked down at him, her face flushed. "I think you're the incredible one."

CHAPTER NINETEEN

AMELIA

Amelia slept like the dead. Their couch sex, coupled with the now-familiar feeling of Daniel asleep next to her, gave her some of the best rest she'd had in a long time. She slept until sunlight was streaming through the curtains.

She eventually opened her eyes when Daniel put a warm hand on her back.

"Your alarm is going to go off soon," he said in a soft voice. "Didn't you set it for seven?"

Amelia groaned. "I'm used to vacation life."

A soft chuckle hit her ears, and his hand rubbed up and down her back. "Would it help if I told you that I made coffee?"

She lifted her head. "Really?"

"I made the one we got at Trader Joe's too."

Memories of her buying a new kind of coffee filled her mind. Plus, the flowers that now sat on her dining room table. It made her cheeks heat.

"Okay, I'll get up." She did so slowly, and she noticed his hair. "You styled it today."

"I can only change so much at one time. I feel . . . nervous."

"I understand." She tilted her head to the side. "You look good either way."

He gave her a smile that made her stomach flip. "Thank you. I also made you some breakfast. You have enough time to enjoy it before we head to work."

He didn't know it, but having breakfast made would make her day so much easier. He gave her a smile and walked back into the living room, and she took her medicine dry so she wouldn't forget it.

The first thing she went for was coffee.

"Do you usually drive in?" he asked.

"No, I take the MARTA. But we can drive in if you want."

"There's a massive wreck on the highway today. So I'd rather not."

She was grateful. She didn't feel like dealing with the building's parking in addition to everyone's reactions to them coming back from vacation together.

It wasn't going to be an easy day. Being a part of office gossip was never her favorite thing, but she couldn't help but remember the way Dana had only talked to *Daniel* when she saw him. She hoped that the knowledge that he was ready to move on didn't make Dana do anything else.

Then, there was the news about what his father had announced. It was another thing that made her dread work. If only she could work from home for just one day to prepare.

"Amelia?" he asked, pulling her out of her thoughts.

"Hm?"

"You're staring at your coffee like it's personally offended you."

"Oh." She huffed out a laugh. "Sorry, I'm just . . . not a morning person."

"I know. But I want to make sure you're okay, especially considering what kind of day it'll be."

"I'll be fine. How bad could it be?"

"Pretty bad," he said. "But you don't have to do this."

Amelia shook her head. "Don't worry about it."

"I don't like you being nervous about something I'm asking you to do."

"It's not you," she said, reaching across the table to grab his hand. "I can handle a little nervousness, okay? I deal with it every day. Anxiety, remember?"

It didn't seem to make him feel any better. "Okay."

She looked at her phone. "The next train leaves soon. We should probably head out."

"Right." Daniel nodded. He stood and she chugged the remainder of her coffee. He eyed her warily. "Doesn't that . . . burn?"

"I'm used to it."

"Your caffeine addiction is scary."

"We all do what we need in order to function," she responded before she threw on her clothes and met Daniel at the door.

The MARTA ride was quiet as usual. The train she took was usually free from any drama and was short. Daniel sat next to her quietly, too, taking in all of the sights.

"What's the plan?" he asked as they got closer to work.

"For what?"

"For how we act at work."

"Right," she muttered. "I think we should have lunch together, but other than that . . . I don't think there is much else we could do. If we oversell this by being super flirty at work, it will look out of place."

"And we could get in trouble if we go *too* far."

"Exactly. We play it cool and make it through the day. That's all we can do."

"Agreed," he said, eyes on their office, which had come into their field of view. Amelia grabbed his hand on instinct, giving him a reassuring smile. When he returned it, her chest loosened. This was a far cry from how they'd been the last time they were in the office, but she wouldn't have it any other way.

They arrived at work right before eight and entered the elevator together. Her hand slipped out of his as he pressed the button for their floor. As she saw the familiar sights of the office, she couldn't help but look at Daniel, who was as put together as always. But now she'd seen *all* of him, and she didn't know how she would go back to being *just* his coworker after this.

Or if she even wanted to.

"Daniel!" a voice called. He held the elevator, and Dana rushed in. "Good morning."

"Morning."

An uncomfortable feeling curled into Amelia's gut, but she ignored it. After yesterday, she didn't know how to feel about Dana's borderline unprofessional questions. She was just his employee, after all.

Dana's eyes glanced over at Amelia, smile dropping for one second. Then her eyes were back on Daniel.

"So," Dana began. "Did you have fun on your trip?"

"We did," he said.

"Where did you go?"

You, Dana had said. She was only talking to Daniel again.

The uncomfortable feeling grew.

"Folly Beach."

"Oh, I love the beach. It's so beautiful and sunny. Plus, I get to wear my favorite swimsuit."

Amelia had to resist the urge to roll her eyes, but then she saw Daniel's eyes on her, a small smile in his expression.

"I'm finding that I love the beach too."

His gaze made her cheeks heat.

"How are you doing?" Dana asked. "You know, with the news about Lucinda being with an older guy?"

Had she not figured out who it was? Maybe something good could happen today.

But Daniel still took it hard. Any trace of a smile disappeared from his face, and Amelia knew Dana had just stomped on a sore subject.

"I'm fine." The elevator door opened. "I'll see you later, Dana." Then he turned to Amelia. "Are we still on for lunch?"

"Of course," she said. "Have a good day."

He nodded and walked toward his office. Dana followed behind but couldn't keep up. Amelia sighed.

This was definitely going to be a long day.

She walked to her own office, closing the door behind her as she entered. She lay against it, alarmed by her legs practically begging her to go talk to Daniel, but she pushed it away and turned on her computer, groaning when she saw two hundred emails in her inbox.

She had work to do.

***

After losing herself to answering emails, Amelia only reappeared from her office to get more coffee. By the time she did, the news had changed.

Andrea was also grabbing a drink, and the moment she saw Amelia, she turned.

"Is Lucinda with Daniel's father?"

Shit. "Um, I shouldn't answer that."

"But she is. It took me a minute to see it, but he called Daniel his son in his Facebook post."

"How did you even see it?"

"Lucinda friend requested a lot of us."

Of course she had.

"It's . . . a long story," she said. "And a sore subject. Daniel is a real person with real feelings, last time I checked."

"Yeah, but he's like a brick wall. He's not going to tell us."

"You don't have to know," Amelia said, shaking her head. "Leave it be."

"Come on. Give us something. You're his girlfriend, right? Or is this just casual?"

"I am his girlfriend," she said sharply. "And honestly, I find it a little weird that you're digging into so much about him."

"This job is boring. We have to have some entertainment."

"Then make up an office game or something."

"You can't tell us anything? Really?"

"I can tell you that I love him and I am there for him. That's all."

She hadn't been sure where the word love came from. But it did the job. Andrea's eyes went wide.

"So it's serious?"

"Very." Her voice was flat. "Now, can I please get my coffee?"

Andrea nodded, seemingly appeased by the morsel of knowledge she had. She ran off, presumably to tell people what she'd learned.

Amelia's mood soured even further. While she knew the rumor mill here was strong, she had underestimated just how pushy people would be for information. She ran back to the safety of her office, not wanting to be questioned again.

She hoped Daniel was okay. He was probably busy answering emails and catching up from his time away too. Plus, he ran a tight ship. Maybe people wouldn't question him as much as her.

At lunchtime, he sent a message through Teams to say he was too busy to leave his desk but ordered something for her. He apologized, saying he would make up for it with dinner.

And he had gone all out with lunch, getting her more than enough for two days' worth of meals. She'd received it only thirty minutes later by delivery and couldn't wait to eat.

It was late in the afternoon, and she hoped no one else would be eating. Thankfully, the break room was mostly empty.

She shoveled her food in her mouth, starving after a long morning.

But then a shadow crossed over her table, and she turned to see her boss, Cheryl. Amelia choked on her food. Cheryl wasn't usually in town. She mostly worked out of a different office.

"Uh, hi," Amelia said after she swallowed her food. "I didn't know you were in town today."

"Oh, I was here for something else and needed an office to come to work in," Cheryl said, and Amelia relaxed a little. "Lots of talk about you today."

"Oh . . . yeah. You know how office gossip is."

"You know, I never thought you and Daniel, of all people, would end up dating."

"There's not a rule against it, right? I did check before all of this happened."

"I'm not here about any rules!" Cheryl said, sitting across from her. She leaned in conspiratorially. "I'm here for *information*. So . . . tell me how it happened."

"Um," Amelia started, trying to get her wits about her. She hadn't expected Cheryl to want to know the details. "Well, we sort of started talking and became friends outside of work. And then we started dating and went on vacation together. It's all . . . boring, really."

"Hm, somehow I doubt it. But I'm sure Daniel has sworn you to secrecy. He's a tough one to crack." Cheryl laughed, and Amelia forced herself to follow. She didn't know how comfortable she felt with her boss pushing her for information. "I mean, if I knew he was into older women, I would have maybe given him a shot. But then again, I'm not like the young women these men go for."

Her forced laugh died off. This was *her* boyfriend.

Well, fake boyfriend.

"You have some stiff competition," Cheryl said. "I've heard some of the younger women in the office talking, and you know how men can be with them."

"I . . . I'm only twenty-eight," Amelia said.

"I mean, of course, that's young in the business world, but the dating world? Yikes. I'm sure it'll be fine, though. Maybe Daniel isn't like other men."

Amelia put down her food, suddenly not feeling very hungry anymore. "I don't think he is."

"After that last wife, though, he has to be looking for an upgrade," Cheryl said. "She was beautiful . . . Not that you're not or anything."

Now her appetite was completely lost. "Thanks."

"Anyway, enjoy your lunch. Just know I'm rooting for you two!" Cheryl replied.

It didn't feel like she was at all. It almost sounded like Cheryl thought Amelia wasn't good enough for Daniel.

And she almost agreed with that.

Amelia got up and walked to the trash can. When she did, she heard the voices of Andrea and Dana—just outside the break room.

"This is my time to make my move," Dana was saying.

"Are we sure he's even over Lucinda? I mean, she's with his *father*."

"He's with Amelia," Dana said. "And we both know that's not going to work out. It's a rebound. It *has* to be."

"You can't blame her, though. She has a chance with someone like *that*? All of us would take it, no matter how short-lived it might be."

"The first relationship after a marriage never works. We all know it."

Amelia stepped back. That was not the opinion she expected to hear. A rebound? *Her*?

She couldn't be. Not with how he looked at her the night before, not with the flowers and the way he talked to her. This had to be more than a measly *fling*.

But it wasn't. This was fake. She couldn't be a rebound because this had an expiration date. Even if they hadn't defined it. The thought made her heart sink, and she wasn't sure why.

CHAPTER TWENTY

DANIEL

Daniel knocked on Amelia's door at five. He'd nearly worked himself to death to get to leave on time, but now all he wanted was to go to her apartment and relax.

She looked up, blinking when she saw him. Her lips pursed, almost as if she wasn't happy to see him.

"I'm sorry about earlier," he rushed to say. "I knew I needed to work through lunch in order to get to leave on time. But we can go now, unless you have more work to do."

"It's fine," she said. "Thank you for the food you ordered. And we can go. I definitely need to." Her tone was short.

"Is everything okay?"

"Yes," she said, but she closed her laptop with more force than usual. "I'm just ready to go home."

"I am too. Let's get out of here."

Their walk to the elevator was quiet, and he could see the sharp edge of her shoulders.

He waited until their office building was behind them before asking her again.

"Are you sure you're okay? You seem tense."

Her gaze stayed on the window, and he wondered if she would even answer him.

"I forgot how catty people can be at work," she said.

"Did someone say something to you?"

"Cheryl was there, and she was . . . weird. She said things about how all the young women in the office wanted you."

"What?"

She finally looked at him. "It made me feel so gross."

"She's never been like that to me, though she did come to my office and ask some questions."

"It was probably some form of girl talk, but I felt like I was not enough somehow."

"Not enough?"

"For you."

"No," he said. "That is absolutely not true. You are more than enough."

"For a fake girlfriend, maybe."

"For a real one. I don't know whoever made you feel like you weren't the kind of woman anyone would be lucky to have, but they're dead wrong. You're as close to perfection as humanly possible."

Her eyes grew wide. "R-really?"

"Yes."

"What about when I get overwhelmed in public?"

"I don't mind that. I get overwhelmed too."

"Or when I need coffee and can't function without it?"

"Coffee is everywhere."

"But—"

"Nothing you say will change my mind," he said.

She blinked, her cheeks darkening. "T-thank you."

"Any time. Did that help?"

"A little, but I think I need time."

"Take all the time you need," he replied. She glanced over at him, biting her lip. Then she laid her head down on his shoulder.

He put his arm around her, tracing gentle patterns into her skin. Every minute that went by, the tension eased from her shoulders.

"So, what do you want for dinner?" she asked, her voice a little lighter as they walked the block to the apartment.

"I owe you dinner, so I'll happily make whatever you want."

She let out a long breath. "I have no idea what I want. But I'm starving."

As they got into the lobby, Amelia's phone chirped. Eyebrows furrowed, she pulled it out.

"Um, Daniel?" she asked. "Is your phone still off?"

"I completely forgot about it, why?"

"I have a Facebook message from Terri asking if I've heard from you."

"My sister?" he asked. "Can I see?"

She turned her phone to him.

Hi, Amelia, I am so sorry to message you like this. I haven't heard from Daniel since Saturday, and with the news that came out yesterday, my mom and I are worried about him. Do you know if he was at work today?

"Oh no," he said. "My phone is in your apartment."

"Let's go get it then."

The moment he turned it on, he was flooded with messages, particularly ones from his mom that grew more and more worried as time went on.

"My family is going to kill me."

"I'll tell Terri you're all right."

"And I'll call my mom." He scrolled through the various messages, seeing a few from his father and Lucinda.

"Oh thank God," his mom said instead of hello. "Are you okay?"

"I'm fine."

"Good. Now I can be mad. Where the hell are you?"

Daniel winced.

"Mom, I'm fine. I'm at . . . ." He looked over at Amelia and remembered he hadn't told his mom what had happened. "I'm out."

"You're out the very next night after your father drops a nuclear bomb on you? With who? I went to your place and Lucinda was there, acting like she was still married to you."

"You went to my apartment?"

"I'm still *at* your apartment!" she said. "I'm outside, anyway. I came because I've been trying to call you ever since I saw what your father announced. I was worried about you."

"I'm sorry," he replied. "I needed some space from my phone after he dropped that massive bomb."

"While I understand that, it doesn't explain where you've been."

He glanced at Amelia.

"I'm with my girlfriend," he replied.

"Promise me it's not Lucinda."

"What? No! I would *never*. Besides, if it were her, I'd be in my apartment right now and you know I'm not there."

She blurted out, "Well how was I supposed to know? She wouldn't let me in the front door!" She hesitated for a moment, her tone a touch lighter. "But with the way she said she was *busy*, it certainly sounds like you two are back together."

"Mom, I *promise*, I'm not with Lucinda."

Amelia grabbed his shoulder. "Invite her over," she whispered.

"What? I—"

"Who is that?"

"Amelia. My girlfriend. I'm staying with her because Lucinda keeps showing up at the apartment."

"You're staying with someone else? Tell me where."

"It's fine. You don't have to—"

"After the scare you just gave me, I need to see you."

Daniel glanced over at Amelia, who looked at him expectantly.

"I'll text you the address."

His mom said her goodbyes before hanging up.

"Is she coming over?" Amelia asked.

"Yep."

"Where is she coming from?"

"My apartment."

"Okay, we only have like . . . fifteen minutes." She looked at her phone. "What's your mom like?"

"She's great . . . when she's not mad. But she's mad right now. I'm sorry this is even happening."

"Why are you apologizing?"

"Because we never talked about bringing my mom into it," he said. "We don't have to do this."

"It's fine," she said, shrugging. "*My* mom's involved."

"You're right. I'm just nervous. Plus, you had a bad day."

"As long as your mom isn't as catty as the people at work, I'll be fine. Besides, you made me feel better. I'm up for it."

"Okay," he said. "I'll make dinner."

"And I'll clean up a little. It'll be fine."

Daniel made a simple dinner of pasta and sauce. The noodles were almost done when there was a loud knock on the door.

Caroline Anderson was a short woman, standing at five foot three, but her personality was far bigger than her body. She had been a single mom for Daniel's entire life, and had single-handedly raised both children once their father decided he wanted to do bigger and better things.

Seeing his mom was comforting after being away for so long. He had been so busy with work that he never made the hour-and-a-half trip to visit her, which he always felt guilty about. The fact that she was in Atlanta by herself meant she had made the drive only not to find him at his apartment, and he couldn't imagine how stressed she was.

"Hi, Mom," Daniel said, hugging her. She smelled like the farm she lived on, which made him miss home. "Thanks for coming by."

"Hi, Daniel," she said, but her voice was still tight. She pulled away and took a good look at him. "You look better than I expected."

He knew that if he had been by himself, he probably would have fallen into a rabbit hole of despair.

"Come in," he offered, moving aside. She stepped into the apartment and took a long look around.

Anyone could tell the difference between Amelia and Lucinda's decoration styles. Lucinda wanted everything to be perfect and clean. She only liked black-and-white pieces that looked good but had no functionality.

Amelia was far more colorful. In more ways than one.

It was then that Daniel could tell his mother was a little shocked. As she surveyed the apartment, her mouth opened and shut as she took it all in.

Amelia came out of her bedroom while his mother continued to stare. She looked a bit disheveled, but when she saw his mom, she smiled at her warmly.

"Hi," Amelia said, a kind smile on her face. "You must be Daniel's mom."

"Hello," his mom replied. "It's nice to meet you. Are you cooking?"

"Daniel is."

"I owed her dinner. Why don't you stay to have some too?"

"I'm sure you two have plans."

"You're welcome here!" Amelia said. "I can only imagine how stressed you've been."

His mom blinked, and he knew she wasn't used to being welcomed by anyone he was dating. Lucinda had never liked her, preferring the company of his father instead.

"I need to drain the pasta," Daniel said.

"I'll help," his mom offered. "I can't let my kid do all the work."

She followed him into the kitchen, and he knew she had questions.

"Where did you find her?"

"I work with her."

Amelia followed them in. "Can I get you anything to drink?"

"Water would be lovely, dear," she said. "I had a long trip to Atlanta."

Amelia nodded and grabbed his mother a glass of water. "Where did you drive from?"

"Oh, I own a farm in southern Tennessee," she replied. "I know it's not fancy or anything, but I love the work."

There it was. His mother knew that her profession wasn't glamorous by any means, and she was used to being judged by Daniel's partners for what she did.

But Amelia's eyes lit up. "You own a farm? By yourself?"

"I do. It's not huge, but it's mine."

"That's amazing! My parents are neighbors of a farm, so I used to help out all the time there as a kid."

"You did?" Daniel asked.

"Oh yeah. I mean, I was terrible at it, but not as bad as John. The photo in the hallway was taken one of the summers that we helped. John looks miserable in it."

Daniel couldn't help it. He turned to go look at it and laughed when he saw John's face. He was covered in mud, wearing overalls, looking angry at the world. Amelia was smiling like she had had the best day of her life.

"I literally keep that to remind John he's terrible at physical labor that isn't gym related," Amelia said.

Daniel's mom had followed him to the photo and she asked, "Is this a pumpkin farm?"

"It is. Lots of people from Atlanta go there every year, so they always needed help getting ready for fall."

"I think I've heard of them," she said, smiling. "It's great that you helped them out."

"If you can even call what I did helping. I was delegated to watering plants."

"Daniel told me you two work together."

"Oh yeah. I'm the director of the HR department."

"You're Amelia Rogers?" she asked.

"Wait, you've heard of me?"

"Daniel told me about you when you got promoted. He was *so* impressed."

He could feel his cheeks heat. He remembered his mom asking about his job. This was when he and Lucinda were really going south, and he had told her about the impressive promotion Amelia had gotten.

"You should be going for a woman like that, Daniel. Someone who is as ambitious and driven as you. Not someone who uses you," his mom had said.

Suddenly, Daniel was embarrassed, and Amelia turned a teasing glance at him.

"Aw, you talked about me to your mom."

"Okay, maybe I did. But you did the same thing."

"*After* we were dating," Amelia said, the lie sounding so real even he believed it. She smirked at him. "We weren't dating when I got promoted."

He didn't have a response to her ribbing, and thankfully, his mom jumped in.

"Oh, I am so glad he found you, dear," she said. "You are just what he needs."

Now Amelia looked embarrassed, and Daniel couldn't help the satisfaction that spread through him at the blush on her cheeks.

"I hope so," she said, her hands tapping on her thighs.

He didn't know why, but Amelia being kind to his mother sent shock waves through him. Lucinda hated anything to do with his mom, and it wasn't until this moment that he realized how much it had affected him.

As Amelia moved to set the table, his mom looked at him with a grin and said, "I really like her."

"I do too." He was surprised by the truth in the words.

As they sat for dinner, his mom told Amelia tales from her farm. She hung on to every word.

Daniel barely talked the whole dinner since his mom dominated the conversation. The only pauses in discussion were immediately filled by Amelia, who would tell his mom stories about her own childhood. He learned a lot at that dinner. Amelia's parents apparently had them work for money every summer helping grow pumpkins, and Mandy always ran the ticket booth in the fall when the farm opened up.

She revealed that she had always thought about having her own farm but never could part with the city to do so. His mom immediately asked Amelia to visit her.

The dinner went on until eight when his mom mentioned she had a long drive ahead of her. Amelia even offered for her to stay overnight, but Daniel knew she had to get home to take care of the animals at the farm before bed. When she pulled Amelia into a long hug, he was certain he'd be asked about her every time he talked to his mother.

"Drive safe," Amelia said. "And let Daniel know when you're home!"

His mom thanked her for being so sweet and then left.

"She's so nice," Amelia said. "I don't know why you were worried at all."

Hearing that she genuinely liked his mother, and was not just putting up a front to appear to, made him stride forward and kiss her right against the door. She let out a squeak, but it didn't take her any time at all to return the gesture.

"What was that for?" she asked as she pulled away. "Not that I'm complaining or anything."

"It was just so nice seeing that you got along with my mother."

She tilted her head to the side, obviously confused. "She's so sweet though."

"You would be surprised at how much Lucinda hated her."

She frowned. "I really wouldn't be. It's her loss anyway."

Daniel smiled and kissed her again. After working all day, he couldn't get enough of her—her smell, the feel of her body in his hands.

Then his phone rang.

"If it's Lucinda or your father, I will kill someone," Amelia said firmly.

Daniel grabbed his phone. "No, it's Terri. She's probably calling to see if I'm dead or not."

"You should answer it," she urged, kissing him on the cheek. "I need to go clean up dinner anyway. Take the bedroom."

He hated leaving her, and his body still felt warm from how she handled the dinner with his mom. But Terri had to be worried since she'd never gotten an update on how he was feeling.

"Hey, Terri."

"Oh, thank God. Where are you?"

"I'm with Amelia."

"Are you okay?"

"Mostly. Yesterday was a lot, so I turned my phone off and forgot to turn it back on."

"I had to message Amelia."

"I know. I was with her when she got it."

Terri let out a breath of relief. "After Dad dropped that bomb, we were worried about you."

"If I'd been alone, it would have been worse. He called too. He asked why I didn't like the post."

"Oh, *come on*. Is he really that ignorant of what he's done?"

"I think so," Daniel replied. "I was thinking about blocking him, actually."

"Really?"

"Yeah, but I know you like updates sometimes."

She was silent for a second. "I only wanted updates when it related to *you*. I couldn't care less about him."

"So you wouldn't mind if I did it?"

"I think you should. You had the right to when he got with Lucinda."

His chest loosened. "Then I'm going to do it. Block him and her."

"Did you really keep in contact with him for me?"

"Yes, mostly. But also, part of me wanted at least an apology."

"But we both know he doesn't do apologies." Her voice was dry. "I'm glad you're doing it, and that Amelia helped you."

"She's even letting me stay at her place since Lucinda keeps coming by the old apartment."

"Really? So, are you guys together now?"

Daniel sighed. "Not officially, but we haven't talked about it being real yet."

"You should. I think she could be good for you."

"Me too. This taste of a life together . . . I could do this forever if she would let me."

"Have you asked her about it?"

"And what if I don't like the answer?"

"Then . . . you don't like the answer."

"That's not what I want to hear."

"But it's the truth." He could practically hear her shrug. "At least you'd know."

"I'll work up the courage to do it. After I block Dad."

"I hope this works out," Terri said, then she cursed. "I have to go. Tommy is climbing the kitchen counter for snacks."

They said their goodbyes. Daniel took a moment to block both his father's and Lucinda's numbers and logged into his Facebook account to block them there too. After he was done, he took a shaky breath, feeling free.

"Everything okay?" Amelia asked as she walked into the bedroom.

"Yes. I'm just finally done with my father."

"How does it feel?"

"Sad, but also good."

She nodded, walking close. She wrapped her arms around him, pulling him into a tight embrace. He let his emotions wash over him for a second, feeling the grief and loss.

But then it faded into a warm glow brought forth by having her close.

"Let's get some rest," she said. "I'm sure we both need it."

"Okay."

"I'll be back after I do the dishes." A shadow crossed over her face.

"I'll do them."

"No!" she said. "I can do this. I have the time, I just . . ."

He grabbed her elbow, quietly leading her away. "You've been stressed. It's okay to relax."

"You're stressed too."

"Yeah, but I don't mind the dishes. If it's something that's hard for you, then it's okay not to do it. I can help."

Amelia blinked quickly, and he thought maybe she was angry at him, but then he noticed her eyes were teary, and he wondered just who had made her feel bad for not being able to get the dishes done.

"Go to bed," he said, kissing her forehead. "I've got this."

"Okay," she said quietly but gratefully.

Daniel finished cleaning up. He was able to clear his mind as his hands moved, which was nice. Lucinda always insisted on having people come in and clean, but he sort of enjoyed it.

When he walked into the bedroom, Amelia was already under the blanket, fast asleep. He smiled at her before he got ready for bed too, excited to join her.

CHAPTER TWENTY-ONE

AMELIA

The next day was a flurry of emails and things to do. Amelia focused as long as she could before there was a knock at her office door.

She looked up and saw Stacey walk in. She bit back a frown at the sight of her coworker, wondering if this was going to be another conversation where she was pushed for information.

"Hi," Amelia said. "What can I do for you?"

Stacey looked nervous. "Um, I just wanted to . . . talk."

"About?"

"You and Daniel."

Amelia immediately felt the urge to go on the defensive, but she kept her voice level. "What about me and Daniel?"

"I just thought you should know that some of the people are saying bad things about you. I know we all talk and everything, but people are going way too far."

"I know," Amelia admitted.

"You know?"

"I'm very quiet in the break room. I heard some of it yesterday."

"Was it Dana?" Stacey asked.

"I . . . can't really answer that."

"I understand," Stacey said. "I feel like she's causing a hostile work environment. I mean, of course it is for you, but not everyone here wants to talk about that. I definitely don't. Yes, it's a surprise you two are dating, but it doesn't involve work. Whatever else is just between you and Daniel."

"While I agree with you, the only thing I can do is tell people to stop, and I doubt that will help."

"I know it doesn't work that way, and I know Cheryl was just as bad as everyone else yesterday. But I wanted you to know . . . not all of us are like that. Not all of us are that interested in your private life." She gave her a shaky smile.

Amelia blinked, shocked at what she was saying. She hadn't thought anyone was on her side since her promotion.

"Thank you," she said genuinely. "It means a lot. Maybe I could try to send an email about it—especially since it's affecting others."

"Most of us will respect it. Maybe not Dana, though."

Amelia couldn't resist the urge to roll her eyes. "I'd imagine not."

"Daniel is her boss. If I were him, I'd be livid. But you totally don't have to tell me anything about it if you don't want to."

"I actually never told Daniel what Dana said."

"Why not?"

"It seems like a personal issue."

"Right, but it's at work too."

"I don't want Daniel to get upset and retaliate."

"I get it. I couldn't even imagine being in your shoes. I mean, you guys just started dating and seeing all of this . . . Ugh."

"Thank you," Amelia said, nodding. "That means a lot."

Stacey smiled and turned for the door. "I guess that's all. I'll see you around."

After Stacey was gone, Amelia took a deep breath, feeling a little bit of tension ease, knowing that at least some people had a good sense of how to be professional.

She was able to focus until noon when she got a message from Daniel.

Daniel: Are you busy? Want to have lunch?

Intrigued, she shut off her computer and walked to his office.

Amelia knocked twice before entering. "Hey," she said.

Daniel smiled at her and gestured to his desk, where two plates of food from the market down the road waited. "I got us food."

"That's really sweet of you," she said as she shut the door. "Don't you want to eat in the break room, though?"

"People never leave me alone if I do that." He rolled his eyes. "Besides, here we have some privacy."

"I think I'd like that." She felt more of her tension melt away.

"How is your day going? Is it any better than yesterday?"

"Kind of." She shrugged. "I was thinking about sending out an email reminding people not to gossip."

"It's probably needed. We really rocked the boat, didn't we?"

Amelia laughed, but his door opened and she immediately stopped. She turned to see who had just barged in. It was Dana, holding a stack of papers.

"Hi, Daniel," she said. "Can you sign this?"

His lips pressed together. "I'm having lunch."

"It's just a quick signature," she insisted.

Amelia made a mental note that if they were going to have lunch together, then they needed to be out of the office entirely. He sighed and signed the papers, but Amelia noticed the way Dana smiled at him, which further plummeted her mood.

"Thanks!" Dana said, walking out without another word toward Amelia. It was like she was invisible.

"See what I mean about being bothered at lunch?"

She wanted to bring up Dana's crush or suggest that they leave the office for lunch so they could continue uninterrupted, but she couldn't manage to do either. So, she smiled and said, "Yep. I definitely do."

"Well, she's good at what she does, so I don't mind."

She felt her mood deflate more. She knew Dana was good at her job—and Daniel respected her for her effort. But just a little over a week ago, that was the exact opinion he'd had of Amelia, and look where they were now. If things were different, would he be more interested in Dana, who she'd heard say she wanted to make a move?

It wasn't a logical thought, but once she had it, it was all she could think about.

"You know what? I think I need to answer some emails," Amelia said, feeling oppressed by everything that was happening.

"Are you sure?"

"Yes, and I don't want to take you away from work. I'll see you tonight."

"Are you okay?" Daniel asked, but his office door opened again, and Dana appeared with more papers to sign. Amelia forced a smile onto her face as she left, thanking him once more for the food.

When she got to her office, she put her head down on the desk and tried not to lose it.

Things were definitely not okay.

CHAPTER TWENTY-TWO

DANIEL

Daniel turned to Dana. She'd once again come to his office right after Amelia had left, giving him more refunds to sign. "You need to go to your direct manager with these. And bring all of them all at once."

"But you're so much easier to talk to."

"I'm busy," he said. "I was trying to have lunch."

"I could always join you."

"No, thank you. I'd rather spend it with my girlfriend."

"But—"

"I'm sending a message to your manager to let her know you'll be going to her." He turned to his computer. She stood there for a few moments longer, but then she finally huffed and left.

Dana was starting to remind him of Lucinda.

He focused on his work, trying not to bother Amelia while she was busy. He stayed in his office, determined not to be disturbed again.

By five thirty, he was ready to leave and stopped by Amelia's office to check in.

"Ready to go?" he asked.

"I can be," she said, not meeting his eyes.

"Is everything okay?"

"Yes. Mostly. I didn't like the interruptions from Dana."

"Neither did I," he replied. "I told her to go to her manager from now on. Hopefully, it won't be a problem again."

"We'll see. But it's fine. I had an unpleasant email in my inbox that I had to deal with."

"We both need to be done for the day," he urged. "Let's go home."

As they got on the train, Amelia yawned, looking exhausted. They stopped to pick up dinner, neither of them feeling up to cooking after the long day.

Instead of relaxing, however, Amelia only seemed to move more and more. She was nervous about something.

"I can't sit still," she muttered. "I think I need to go to the gym to work out this energy."

"That's a great idea. Do you mind if I go too?"

"I should warn you that I get really red-faced when I work out. It's not a pretty sight."

"I think I can deal with that," he replied.

"We'll see. But you're welcome to come. We could go to the gym John works at. Maybe he'll be there."

"That would be great."

Amelia changed into leggings and a tank top, and Daniel made a mental note that he needed workout clothes from his apartment if he was going to be making a habit of this.

This time, they drove, but it was past rush hour, so traffic was at a minimum. The gym was busier than he expected, but John was there, working with someone else.

The moment he saw them, he waved, a smile crossing his face.

"Let's warm up," Amelia said. "Maybe we can talk to him after he's done."

They walked on the treadmill for five minutes before moving to the weights area. After they'd done a few exercises, John joined them.

"Hey, you two," he greeted. "I didn't expect to see you here."

"We needed a good workout," Amelia said. "Are you busy?"

"My client is going to be late, so I could give you a workout that will kick your ass."

"I think I need it. I can't sit still for shit. It was a rough day at the office."

"And I'm always happy to work out," Daniel added.

"Then let's do this." John gave them a list and provided a quick tutorial on how to do each of them. By the time he was working with his next client, Daniel could already tell that he'd be sore.

"He doesn't take it easy on anyone," Amelia huffed after finishing a set. "Not even family."

It was hard—harder than he'd ever worked out before, but he got breaks when Amelia used the machine for her reps.

They were both dripping with sweat by the time they were done. Daniel went to the men's locker room to splash water on his face.

"Was that enough of an ass kicking for you?"

Daniel turned, seeing John coming out of the bathroom. "Yeah," he replied. "It was hard."

"Good. I hope it helped Amelia."

"I think so," Daniel said. "Work has been hard on her."

"It always is. Even when she was in school she struggled."

"Really?"

"Yes, but you didn't hear that from me."

"Would she have a problem with me knowing?"

"Her ex hurt her in more ways than one. She's slow to trust, but I think you're perfect for her. Just give her time."

"I'll give her all she needs."

"And that is why I like you. Hopefully, you don't hate me too much for the workout."

"No, I needed it. Maybe I'll come back in a few days when the inevitable soreness wears off."

***

The next morning, Daniel was as sore as expected. He was slow to move, though Amelia didn't seem to share the sentiment.

"Are you even hurting at all?" he asked with a groan.

"No. I'm guessing you are?" She raised an eyebrow.

"I think I'm dying."

She laughed at him and dragged him out of bed.

He complained until she got a hot shower going and practically pushed him into it. Once he felt a little better, they had a quick breakfast before going to work. They went their separate ways when they got in, but she was on his mind the whole morning.

When Daniel heard a knock at his door, he hoped it was her. However, he was disappointed to find only Dana.

"What can I do for you?" he asked, resisting the urge to sigh.

"My manager is on break, so I have more refunds for you to sign," she said. He gritted his teeth and took them from her. If he got this over with, then she'd leave him alone. "So, how are you and Amelia doing?"

Or not.

"Does this have to do with work?"

"Not every conversation has to be about work."

"It does when you work for me."

"But it just seems so weird . . . You know, with it being so soon."

"I don't know what you expect me to say, Dana. I don't talk about my private life at work." His voice was stern.

"But you do with Amelia," she said.

"*Amelia* isn't my employee." He could feel his frustration building. "*You* are. Let this go."

"But—"

"Dana," he warned. "I do not want to take disciplinary action against you, but I will."

She seemed to deflate, and she said, "Right, sorry."

She then walked out. He let out a long breath, frustrated with her attempts to push him into an answer. He'd never seen her like this, and he didn't want to again.

But the threat seemed to work. He was left alone for most of the day, which was needed, considering he had multiple meetings.

At five, Amelia knocked on his door.

"I'm so ready to get home," she said, her voice tight. "I'm not focusing very well."

"I'm done too. Sorry, I missed lunch again. I'll take you out to dinner to make up for it."

"That sounds perfect," she replied.

They took the MARTA to a nearby restaurant, a nicer one that he hoped Amelia would like. Once there was food on the table, her mood got better.

When they got home, they had time to watch a little bit of TV before she fell asleep on his shoulder. He put her in bed and then tidied up the house.

He was folding a blanket when he knocked Amelia's purse on the ground. He bent down to pick it up, only to see a pill bottle fall out, the name side facing him. The last thing he wanted to do was pry, but he'd never heard of it, and his heart sank. What if she'd been keeping a serious illness from him?

He looked it up and saw it was an ADHD medication.

For a moment, he was relieved. It made sense. She had trouble focusing and getting things done, but why would she not have told him about it?

He could have put his phone down then, but he didn't. If Amelia was on something for it, then there had to be a reason. And maybe one day, she would need help with it. When he searched for ADHD, he found all the traditional symptoms—not being able to sit still, not being able to focus. But it was all geared for kids, not adults.

So he typed in a search for adults, and then a suggested search read *ADHD in adult women*.

That was what he clicked on.

And then he realized ADHD was more than he thought.

He read through everything, feeling like he had been hit by a train. ADHD came with a laundry list of things that could go wrong. Many of the symptoms were different in women. They tended to have poorer friendships, to be messier, and often treated it with self-medicated drugs. It encompassed everything, from their social life to their monetary life. It could easily get dangerous while driving and dangerous for addiction. It meant anything from vastly overeating to ignoring bodily needs.

He had no idea how much it affected a person's everyday life.

Through his search, he found people debating the use of medication, especially those that were labeled controlled substances. Many of the comments on the forum called people using it *weak* or *addicted*.

Had this been what her ex had done?

He put the bottle back. Just how bad had Andrew hurt her? And was it tied to the reason she hadn't told him?

For as many questions as he had, he also knew he didn't want to push her into telling him until she was ready. She was already stressed with work, and he didn't want to make it worse.

Hopefully, she would open up to him about it, and when she did, he would be there for her.

CHAPTER TWENTY-THREE

AMELIA

Amelia woke up and her mind was racing. She hated it when she got like this. It only happened when stress was piling up, much like her email inbox had been the last few days.

People weren't taking the gossip reminder well, and she still got curious glances or cruel glares in the hallway. On top of that, there was an employee who wasn't happy about their allotted breaks, and she'd been the one to deal with the mediation for it.

Her medicine could stop a lot of things, but it didn't fix it all. And when her brain ran wild, it didn't matter that she was on it, her mind would never stop.

It was going to be a long day.

And worse, Daniel would probably notice.

"Hey," he greeted her in a soft voice. "We'll need to get ready to go soon."

She groaned. The day had barely begun and she was already exhausted.

"I made you coffee and breakfast."

"Thank you," she said, forcing herself to get up. After a cup of it and her food, Daniel disappeared to the bedroom. There was something she needed to do, but she couldn't remember what. Instead, she followed him to get ready as well.

By the time they were done, he kissed her on the cheek. The action sent butterflies down to her stomach, which then prompted her brain to remind her that this was fake and that he wouldn't stay after he knew about her ADHD, and how much she wanted him around forever.

Daniel offered to drive into work, asking if she wanted anything else before they went to the office. The kindness brought tears to her eyes because he was so sweet, and she was going to miss this when he was gone.

The food helped her mood, but her brain was still a mess. She talked in circles, and she could tell he was having a hard time following her. When she got to work, she struggled to read emails. She got extra coffee, knowing it would help, and was maybe able to squeeze a few minutes of focus out of her brain. She had to pause and restart tasks a million times that day, which made everything more and more frustrating.

On her third walk of the day, she went up to the break room. She ran into Stacey, who was holding her face in her hands at a table. Amelia stopped when she saw her and then considered leaving Stacey to deal with whatever she was going through.

But that didn't feel right, so she walked up and sat next to her.

"Hey, are you okay?"

Stacey looked up with wide eyes. They were red-rimmed.

"Oh, God," Stacey said, her voice thick. "I know I should be working. I'll get back to it."

"No," Amelia said. "I wasn't asking you to get back to work. What's wrong?"

She seemed to consider what she wanted to say. "My boyfriend is cheating on me."

"Oh. Oh no. I'm so sorry."

Her brain gave her a dozen other things she could say, ranging from, *"Why would he cheat on someone so nice?"* to *"Kill him."*

But none of it was helpful.

"It's okay. He's been distant but . . . I found out last night, and right now, he's packing up his things." Stacey laughed humorlessly. "He sent me a photo of our apartment . . . It's nearly empty."

Amelia placed her hand on Stacey's shoulder. "That's terrible."

She took a shaky breath. "It wasn't going to work out anyway, but I just couldn't deal with work stuff while I was upset."

Amelia could definitely relate.

"Why don't you take the day off?" she offered.

"I can't just leave," Stacey said. "I'm needed here."

"Yes, but taking a day off will be better for you in the end. And besides, I'm literally the director of HR. And I give you permission."

"Are you sure?"

Amelia nodded, giving her a warm smile. Stacey's face was awash with gratefulness.

"Thank you," she said. "I think I'm going shopping. It might make me feel better."

"Get some new furniture while you're at it," Amelia encouraged. "I hear HomeGoods has a sale, or hell, even IKEA. Plus, the meatballs are amazing. You should go."

Stacey nodded and stood from the table. She looked to be in better spirits. Amelia felt good about getting her to go home, and then it hit her that maybe she needed to take her own advice.

But not today. She needed to at least get something of substance done before she left.

She made her coffee before walking back to her office. She glanced toward where Daniel's office was and saw Dana walking toward it.

It did not help her mood.

In the deep, dark parts of her mind, she wondered if maybe he was interested in Dana in some way. She had no evidence, but *what if*? Maybe now that he'd gotten over Lucinda, everyone was fair game. Maybe someone else in the office was better than Amelia.

And that thought lingered throughout the day.

It didn't help that Daniel stayed late, and she was tempted to see if Dana stayed late as well, but she was far more professional than that.

So, she went home and tried not to think about it.

But her anxiety was high, and she tried to clean the apartment, doing everything she could to distract herself. It worked for a bit, until it didn't.

It was both a benefit and a curse that her brain worked so fast. When she was in control of it, she could get so much done. But on bad days, it was like she was snowballing down a hill with no brakes. She would find the worst thing to think about and then never let it go. It was like picking at a wound.

And it was exactly what she was doing now. Even while she was cleaning, all the things she didn't want to think about—Dana and Daniel, and even Andrew—were all at the forefront of her mind.

She knew Daniel wasn't like Andrew, yet she was terrified he was. She knew she needed to tell him about her ADHD, but she couldn't. She knew he would never date a subordinate, but her mind saw it anyway.

At seven, Amelia lay on her couch and sighed. There was nothing else to do, and she felt like she was losing it trying to avoid everything, and the last thing she needed was to still be acting off while Daniel was here.

She wasn't sure what to do with herself, so she decided to go on a run.

There was a two-mile path that she loved to take. It had hills and plenty of turns to keep her interested. She had about an hour and a half before the sun set for the day, so she pushed herself and hoped she would be back before eight.

She seriously didn't think that Daniel would even have come home by then. He seemed so busy.

As she ran, the challenge of it forced her to only think about the road in front of her. This was exactly what she needed, and she was so into it that she turned her phone off, just to make sure she wouldn't be tempted to check social media—a habit that always made her feel worse about herself.

Amelia beat her goal of getting back by eight by five minutes. She felt exhausted and her legs ached but in a good way. She knew she had done the right thing.

She leisurely checked her mail as she took the stairs to her apartment, feeling better than she had all day. She unlocked her door, thinking of a bath, when she saw a shadow in her living room that made her nearly scream.

"There you are," Daniel said, his voice laced with annoyance. "Where were you?"

Amelia stared at him for a long moment. She had been so focused on her run that she had totally forgotten that he was even staying with her.

"I was running."

"I texted you five times and you never answered."

"I turned off my phone to focus. It was a rough day."

His eyes softened, but she knew she had still annoyed him by not being home.

Anxiety crawled down her back.

"I didn't know where you were."

"I didn't know when you were coming home," Amelia replied, feeling a bit defensive, but she forced out a breath of air and tried to let it go. "I'm sorry."

He paused for a long moment. His face was set in a frown, and she could feel all of the worry of her day come back at her.

"You've been off today. What's going on?"

She wasn't sure how to answer that. Her mind filed through the day, like a mail sorter who was two days behind, and the worst words came out of her mouth.

"What do you think about Dana?"

He blinked. "I don't think anything about her, other than I've told her to let me work."

"But like . . . if you *had* to."

"The only way I think about her is as my employee. Nothing else."

"But—"

"Amelia, there is nothing else."

His voice was firm, and she felt like an idiot. "It's just . . . you can have anyone. And after Cheryl saying you would go after a younger, prettier woman, and the fact that I overheard them talking shit about me—"

"Hang on. Who was talking about you?"

"Dana and Andrea. They said that I was only a fling and the first relationship after a marriage never works out, which is so insulting, by the way."

"She—" he nearly snapped, but then he took a deep breath to calm himself. *Shit.* He was mad at her. "Why didn't you tell me?"

"Because I didn't want you upset with her over something personal."

"Personal or not, that is incredibly inappropriate for her to say."

"Yeah, I'm aware," she muttered. "But I can't just snap my fingers and make her stop. I sent out that email, all right? That's about all I can do."

"I can talk to her."

"No, I don't want you doing that."

"Why not?"

"Because I don't want personal issues messing with work. You said she's a good employee so there's no need to mess that up just because she's being petty."

"You're my girlfriend. I have a right to defend you against that kind of stuff."

"*Fake* girlfriend," she reminded. "Which is why I shouldn't have even been upset. We're *supposed* to end."

Daniel shook his head. "Is that really what you think? That there is some version of this where I leave you at the end of it?"

She blinked, heart pounding. "I don't know why you would stay."

And she didn't. She'd messed up today by not being home when he was. She couldn't form a decent thought to save her life, and she'd made him angry by bringing up Dana. She'd screwed up at every turn.

"I have a million reasons why I would stay."

"But—"

"Amelia, I want this to be real."

"But it's not."

Annoyance crossed his face again, and another voice spoke.

"God, Amelia. Everything going wrong in this relationship is because of you!"

"Are you saying that because you don't want it to be real?" Daniel asked.

"No . . . I mean . . . I don't know."

"Answer me, Amelia. Why can't you just figure it out for once in your life?"

"I just need to know what you expect of me. And if this will only ever be fake to you."

Amelia didn't answer. She couldn't.

"Please, I just need an answer."

But she was no longer in her apartment. She was back at her old place, the one she shared with Andrew.

"Answer me," Andrew demanded. "Answer me right now."

"I don't have an answer, okay? I'm having a hard time right now with my—"

"What? With your ADHD?" The words were said mockingly. "You blame everything on that shit, Amelia. Grow up!"

"But it's what's going on!"

"Ugh! I'm sick of it!" Andrew yelled. He had been facing away from her, but he grabbed his phone, turned, and hurled it at her.

A hand grabbed her arm and she screamed, covering her head to protect her from an object heading right for her.

Then there was silence.

No phone hit the wall. No hands touched her and no objects shattered. Andrew didn't continue yelling and throwing other things.

Nothing happened because she wasn't in the old place anymore.

Daniel was standing in front of her, but he took a step back, his eyes wide. He looked at her like she was . . .

Crazy.

"Oh God." Amelia sank to the floor, shaking as she remembered the last night she and Andrew had ever spent together. She put her hands over her face, unable to meet Daniel's eyes.

She had been scared that he was going to *hit* her, of all things—that he was going to be like Andrew, who blamed everything on anyone he could find. She'd screamed as if Andrew had approached her, not Daniel.

He was silent, and she couldn't expect anything else out of him. She was surprised he was even still in the apartment after what he'd just seen.

But it had been like she was back there, that specific night. All she could see was the terrible memories playing out over and over again.

And it hit her then. She'd heard of this before. *PTSD*. She never imagined she could have it, but she'd never been in a position like this before, arguing with someone she cared about because deep down, she'd been afraid of this happening.

And now it was going to push Daniel away.

Andrew had ruined her. That was just another thing to add to the laundry list of issues she had, issues that made her entirely wrong for anyone. Why would Daniel *ever* want to be with someone who was a basket case like she was, especially after leaving someone like Lucinda?

She wasn't keeping her breath slow, and soon, she felt the tingling in her hands and the numbness in her face that told her she was having a panic attack.

"Amelia," Daniel started. "Do you want me near you?"

She couldn't answer. Her hands pressed into her face tighter.

"J-just go," she managed to choke out. "You don't have to stay for this."

"No," he said, which surprised her. She looked at him, and he was kneeling in front of her. "I'm not leaving you."

"You should. You should run and never look back."

"That's something a coward would do," he said. "But I'm here, next to you, even when you're not perfect. I will never run from you, Amelia. I'll be the one running *to* you."

He was lying. He *had* to be lying. No one would want to sit there and deal with someone who was an emotional mess and couldn't get it together.

Except her dad.

Her mom.

John.

Daniel gently reached and brushed away a tear. She surprised herself by letting him.

"I'm not going anywhere."

She could only stare at him. Her mind finally quieted, her breathing slowed, and the post-anxiety exhaustion hit her.

Amelia said thickly, "I think . . . I think I have PTSD."

"From what?"

She looked at him. "Andrew. The last night we were together, he snapped and threw his phone at me. When I tried to pick it up, he . . ." She couldn't say it, but she could *feel* it.

"He hit you, didn't he?"

"Y-yes," she choked out. "I left him after that. But the damage was done."

He took a long, deep breath. When she looked up, his lips were pursed.

"You're mad."

"Of course I am. I don't want anyone hurting you. Whether it's someone petty like Dana and Andrea, or if it's more serious."

"B-but maybe I deserved—"

"You didn't deserve it, no matter what you did."

"Daniel . . . I . . ." She stopped herself from trying to figure out what she was going to say. "I'm . . . I'm messed up. I can't remember things. I get behind on chores. I can't focus or sit still."

"None of that means you're messed up."

"I have ADHD. The me you see is only because I have to take medicine every day. I literally can't function without it."

She hadn't told anyone since Andrew, and the words cracked as they came out. She looked back down at her hands and waited for Daniel to say he was leaving or that maybe she had deserved it this entire time.

"I know."

"What? How did you know?"

"Because last night, I knocked your purse over and saw the medicine."

"But . . . but I'm on a generic ADHD medication—not a known one. How would you know?"

"Google," he said. "I didn't know if it was for a heart problem or something I needed to know about."

"And it didn't change anything?"

"Other than me giving you space to take your medication and being sure you ate after taking it so you wouldn't be sick, then no. None of it changes a thing."

"O-oh," she said. "But I didn't . . . *shit,* I forgot to take it. No wonder I've felt like garbage today."

Unneeded words filtered through her mind.

"So, this is the real you, then? Not all dumbed down by medication?"

"You don't even need this poison."

It was Andrew, haunting her once again.

Daniel stood and went to her purse, grabbing the bottle. She watched him, trying to think of ways to get it refilled if he threw it out.

"Here," he said, holding it out to her with her bottle of water.

"What are you doing?"

"You need to take it. I'm sorry if me being here has made you feel like you couldn't, but it's good for you to be on what you need to function."

Amelia reached out slowly with shaky hands and grabbed the bottle. She gripped it tight in her fist. "I . . . I'll have to take it in the morning. It'll keep me up all night if I take it too late. But t-thank you. I appreciate it." She smiled.

"Then what *would* help? Dinner?"

"You're not mad?"

"About what?"

"About me needing medication."

"Absolutely not," he replied. "I mean . . . I wish I had known sooner, but I get why you didn't tell me. I figured it was the ex. I just didn't know how bad it was."

She wiped at her face, embarrassed. "Yeah. He was . . . awful. He didn't believe in how much the medication was necessary for me to function. He'd make fun of me for needing it, and then when I wasn't on it, I started showing symptoms, and I mean the nuanced ones, like forgetting the dishes, or not being able to listen, or going on tangents . . ." She blushed. "Like I'm doing now."

Daniel's lips pressed together. "Amelia, it's fine. All of it is. He's the one who was wrong."

"I know," she said. "And it's not like I believe him now. It's just . . . I grew up with this amazing family, and Andrew was so different, and he would say everyone thought like he did. So, I assumed that *my family* was different. Maybe everyone else *was* like him, so it became easier to just hide it. And then with dating, I didn't think I could trust someone again."

"And how do you feel now?"

"I'm starting to think I trust you," she said.

"I'm honored you do." He brushed a hand over her wet cheek. "And I'll do my best to make sure you *never* feel like you're not enough again. You're safe when you're with me. I can't promise no one will ever hurt you, no matter how much I might want to, but I can promise that I'll do my best to make sure it's never *me* who does it."

"Why?"

"Because I love you, and that means I am with you through all of it, never against you. And if you don't feel the same way, that's fine, but I just hope that one day you do."

She couldn't help the laugh of disbelief that came out of her mouth. "You're kidding."

"I'm not kidding," he said. "I'm telling you the truth."

She stared at him, trying to find signs of a lie.

She didn't find any.

"But . . . What if I don't do the dishes?"

"I can do them."

"What if I need therapy again . . . like every week?"

"I'll drive you to the appointments."

"What if I have to change medication, and I get all annoying and loud, or talk in circles when I'm really trying to say something simple?"

"That's fine. I love you for everything you are, ADHD and all, because you're still *you*. Even when you're struggling. You're always Amelia, and that's who I love. I would do it all for you if you would let me."

She stared at him, her mind a jumbled mess. It sounded too good to be true. This had to be a dream.

But it wasn't. She had seen real, healthy love before. In her mom and dad. This was what her dad preached. This was what helped her mom keep a level head all these years.

Daniel was here. He knew, and he wasn't scared. He didn't think she was lying. He didn't think she was weak or stupid for needing the medication. He was just *here*.

"Okay," she said, her voice soft and broken but still hers. "Please stay. I can't let you do it *all*, but I know I need help."

His lips turned upward. "And I will definitely do that."

"And for the record?"

"Yeah?"

"I love you too."

His smile only grew. "Is it okay if I kiss you now?"

"Yes," she breathed. "Please."

Daniel leaned forward, capturing her lips with his. And now, with all of her secrets out in the open, it felt like things were finally in their proper place.

There was nothing fake about them anymore. From now on, it would only be real.

EPILOGUE

AMELIA

One Year Later

Amelia's day was going by painfully slowly.

She had everything done for a week ahead. The bags were packed, the fridge was clean and empty of all perishable items, and her email inbox was empty.

She surveyed her apartment, feeling accomplished.

Ever since she left her last job, she had been remotely working from her apartment. Leaving the company where she had met Daniel was a hard choice, but she knew it was the right one. She didn't fare well with gossip, and the inappropriateness of Cheryl had gotten too much to handle. She never thought she could deal with working from home, but everything seemed to have fallen into place when she changed her medication to something a little better suited for her type of ADHD.

Daniel had been nothing but supportive in the last year. True to his word, he drove her to appointments and supported her when changing to the new medication. And she was glad that she had. It was so much easier to keep herself organized.

Interestingly, it was he who was now falling behind on organization, at least at work. With the merger of another billing office at their old company, he was busier than ever, and Amelia knew he was lucky to be able to take a week off with everything going on.

He had been trying to find a job somewhere else. The addition of responsibilities didn't come with a pay raise, and he didn't get much support from corporate when he had to fire Dana for continuing to be inappropriate at work. He was tired of the hours and tired of the gossip too.

He had a few interviews lined up, and hopefully, one of them would work out. But first, he needed a break from the office.

Since he was working late, again, Amelia had made plans with Stacey that afternoon to get out of the apartment.

After she left her last company, Stacey reached out, hoping to become friends now that Amelia wasn't her boss. It worked out great. Having a friend in town made everything easier.

Stacey also lived close by. She had left their company for a tech job in the city that paid significantly more, so they were within walking distance of each other. She always came by when she had a free minute, and they would walk through the underground mall or grab coffee when they had the time.

"Are you ready for your vacation?" Stacey asked when Amelia opened her apartment door.

She gestured to the bags in the entryway. "I've never been more prepared in my life."

"Isn't working from home great?" Stacey asked. "You have so much more time to get things done."

Amelia laughed. "It also helps that I *feel* like getting things done. Daniel was *so* right when he said I should try something else."

She had finally worked up the nerve to share her mental health journey with Stacey, and her friend didn't even flinch at the news. Surprisingly, she had been in the middle of getting a diagnosis herself.

And now that she had a better support group, her mental health wasn't shameful anymore. It was just a fact of her life.

The women caught up while they walked through downtown. They first stopped for coffee on the way to the mall, and when they got there, they looked around the shops.

Amelia wound up buying a dress from one of the local sellers. It was a bright red number with cutouts on the sides that showed off her midsection. Stacey had told her it would be a crime if she didn't get it. Usually, Amelia would have said no. She never had anywhere to wear a pretty dress.

But maybe on this vacation, she would.

"Has Daniel put two and two together?" Stacey asked.

"Not yet," Amelia said. "For once in my life, I think I've actually been smooth."

"Do you have it?"

She smiled and brought out the box in her bag. It was a simple titanium band. "It came in a few days ago."

"I can't believe you're going to be the one to propose."

"Apparently, Lucinda had made her proposal a whole affair. It's only fair if I do it."

When they last talked about marriage, Daniel had been for it but hadn't brought it up since. He'd said he wanted things to be low-key since Lucinda had expected the world and more. Amelia figured her planning the proposal was the perfect idea.

She only hoped he said yes.

"So, who is this date you have tonight?" Amelia asked, content to change the subject. She'd get nervous if she thought about it too long, and that was the last thing she needed.

"Oh, he's just some guy my mom set me up with. I doubt it's going to go well."

"Don't think of it like that," Amelia said. "If you do, then it definitely won't go well."

"I suppose . . . . I guess I'm still down on my luck in the romance department. It's easier to think of it this way. It doesn't get my hopes up too high."

"Romance is great when you have the right person."

"I know. I'm just waiting on my own perfect man. But I doubt I'll be able to top you faking a relationship to get your family off your back."

Stacey had been floored when she found out the truth, but Amelia was glad that someone finally knew. One of these days, she'd have to let her family in on the secret. Her mom remained ecstatic that Amelia and Daniel were still together, and she didn't want to let them know that, technically, it was newer than they thought.

Amelia and Stacey hung out until seven when Daniel texted her that he was leaving work. They walked back to the apartment, waiting for him to arrive.

"Hey," he said to both of them. "Have a good day at the mall?"

"It was fine," Stacey said. "This one wasn't too damaging to the bank account."

Amelia rolled her eyes and gestured to her one bag. "I just got a new outfit."

Stacey gave her a look that said it wasn't *just* an outfit but a sexy dress she was going to propose to her boyfriend in. But Amelia ignored it. She had made it this far without letting her plans slip out. It wouldn't happen now.

"Ugh," Stacey said, checking her watch. "I need to get back before my dog pees on the floor again. I'll see you guys next week. Be safe!"

After Stacey was gone, Amelia gave Daniel a kiss and asked, "How was your day?"

He groaned. "Terrible, but the last day before vacations always is. I can't wait to relax for a little bit."

"Me either, but first, we should eat before hauling all of our luggage to the car. I'll even cook."

"What did I ever do to deserve you?"

There was plenty that he'd done, but he knew that. She never stopped thanking him for all of his support.

She went to the kitchen to cook dinner and think about her plans to propose. Daniel took a shower to relax.

When he came out, his hair was curly and wet, his features more relaxed. "I canceled my therapy for this coming week. Did you cancel yours?"

"Yep. I sent the email last week." She smiled at him.

They both went twice a month: him for his issues with Lucinda and his father, and Amelia for her PTSD. It had been hard to admit they both needed to go, but they agreed it was necessary after accidentally triggering past memories for each other one too many times.

After dinner, Daniel took the bags out to the car, and they finished up the last remaining items on the list.

They had been living together since before they technically even started dating. He never saw the point of leaving after they agreed to be together. He simply paid the remaining two months of rent to satisfy the lease of his old place and spent his time selling his stuff from his old apartment. He wound up giving Lucinda's leftover outfits to John, who, in exchange, gave him free training sessions for all the clothes.

Daniel had traded in the Miata for a different car, but they rarely drove it, considering they rode together all of the time. Amelia's place had slowly become Amelia and Daniel's place, with pictures of both of their pasts adorning the walls, and all their stuff shoved into closets.

Now that they had two people living there and both of them might be working from home soon, they had discussed moving farther from town and getting somewhere bigger, but Amelia knew she was going to have a hard time leaving this place. It was where many good memories were made.

But even Amelia could admit they had outgrown it. Daniel had gotten back in touch with some of his college friends, and she had called her one old friend a few times. They needed a guest room now that their social circle had grown.

None of that mattered, though, since they were heading to the beach with Amelia's family in the morning. They had a week away, and they knew they were going to use every second of it.

***

The next morning, Daniel and Amelia both took turns driving to the beach. She had gotten used to driving since she had changed her medicine, and it wasn't nearly as stressful as it used to be.

They arrived first and kept themselves busy with sightseeing and walks. When her parents and John got there, they all exchanged long, excited hugs.

Daniel and Amelia's family had kept in good contact. They had known that he wasn't going anywhere since they had left the beach a year prior, and he had grown close with them. Once a week, they met up with John to work out, and her parents had joined them for many lunches in the city.

Amelia couldn't help but notice how different he was from who he was a year ago. He had grown into himself, becoming more confident over the twelve months of their relationship. It only cemented just how much she wanted to spend the rest of her life watching him grow, and she was ready to commit to it.

They spent the first night catching up at dinner, all talking about their daily lives.

Just like their first night on the last trip, they went for a romantic night walk. When she put on her new dress, Daniel nearly tripped over himself looking at it.

"*That's* what you and Stacey got?"

"Yes," Amelia said, blushing. "Is it too much? I can change."

"No, it's beautiful. Please don't change. Please *never* change."

She pulled him into a kiss, and she was tempted to let it go further, but she knew she had a proposal to get through first.

He grabbed her hand as they walked down to the beach, and she knew this was the perfect time to propose. And even if he said no, she trusted he would give her a good reason for it.

Her palms were sweaty, though, especially the one she held Daniel's hand with, but she wasn't going to chicken out, not when she wanted this so much.

Come on, she told herself. *You got this. Just get down on one knee.*

"Hey, Amelia?"

Shit. He was going to ask her if she was okay. And she couldn't lie about her nerves, but she couldn't tell him the reason either, unless she wanted to forgo the whole proposal.

He cleared his throat, and she turned, her jaw dropping as she saw *him* with a ring box and on one knee.

"What . . . what are you doing?" she asked, feeling a little breathless.

"I rehearsed this in my head. So just listen, okay?"

She could only blink in shock.

"Amelia, you are my best friend and the greatest person I could ask to share my life with. I never thought I would get married again, but you changed everything for me, and I want to ask if you would . . . if you would marry me."

He opened the box, revealing the most beautiful engagement ring she had ever seen. It was a ruby, something completely unorthodox, and a simple band with intricate leaf designs on the side.

And it was silver, matching the one she had gotten for him perfectly.

"I can't believe this," she said, happy tears in her eyes.

"In a good or a bad way?"

She laughed despite the tears streaming down her cheeks and reached into her dress's secret pocket to pull out her ring for him. "You stole my idea."

Daniel laughed too. "You were going to propose?"

"Yeah," she said. "That's why I was so nervous. I thought you would catch me."

"No, *I* was nervous. We really were going to propose at the same time?"

"I think so."

Amelia giggled at their ridiculous situation first, which sent Daniel into a fit of laugher too.

"So it's a yes, right?" he asked the moment he could speak again.

"Duh," she replied. "What about you? Are you willing to marry me?"

"Any day." He smiled up at her. She offered her hand to him, and he slid the ring on.

When they got back to the condo, her mom screamed and frantically hugged them both. Her dad welcomed Daniel to the family officially, and John gave them hugs and asked who was taking whose name.

It was an easy choice. And a year later, when she walked down the aisle, they became Daniel and Amelia Rogers.

WANT MORE?

G et the bonus chapter where Amelia and Daniel tell their family of their fake relationship

THANK YOU

This was the novel written right after *Failure to Thrive*, and it means so much to me to have it edited and back out into the world. As a person with ADHD myself, I experienced the opposite of what Amelia did, where my parents didn't believe in it, but my partner did. I have been so lucky to be surrounded by people who have always helped me with my mental illness. And while Amelia didn't have some of the same struggles I did, I was happy to write a character with supportive and kind parents.

Thank you to my readers for letting me share my stories. Thank you to Kasey for always editing these and making them better. And thank you to Lizzie, Josh, and the rest of my support system for supporting me while I follow my dreams. I know I say this each time, but I really wouldn't have been able to do this without each and every one of you.

ABOUT THE AUTHOR

Elle Rivers writes fun romance books filled with real-world problems wrapped in beautiful, heartwarming happy endings. When not writing, she can be found speed-reading other authors' amazing romance novels, curling up next to any warm object she can find, or singing obnoxiously loud to Taylor Swift.

Elle was born and raised in Nashville, TN, and she considers herself one of the few native Nashvillians who does not like country music. She has eight cats who fight for the spot on her lap, and eight chickens who couldn't care less about her unless she is bringing them food. She lives with her romance hero of a husband who endlessly supports her writing endeavors, and her son, who is the biggest, but most adorable, distraction.